No Killer Has Wings
The Casebook of Dr. Joel Hoffman

Other book collections by Arthur Porges:

Three Porges Parodies and a Pastiche (1988)
The Mirror and Other Strange Reflections (2002)
Eight Problems in Space: The Ensign De Ruyter Stories (2008)
The Adventures of Stately Homes and Sherman Horn (2008)
The Calabash of Coral Island and Other Early Stories (2008)
The Miracle of the Bread and Other Stories (2008)
Spring, 1836: Selected Poems (2008)
The Devil and Simon Flagg and Other Fantastic Tales (2009)
The Curious Cases of Cyriack Skinner Grey (2009)
The Ruum and Other Science Fiction Stories (2010)
The Rescuer and Other Science Fiction Stories (2014)
Unusual Plants of the Galaxy (2014)

Forthcoming titles by Arthur Porges:

The Price of a Princess: Hardboiled Crime Fiction
Collected Essays: Volume One
Collected Essays: Volume Two

Books by F. W. Thomas (from the same publisher):

Tales From Stonecutter Street (2010)
Star Turns (2011)
The Rising Sap (2013)

Books by Basil Wells (from the same publisher):

Final Voyage and Other Science Fiction Stories (2016)

No Killer Has Wings
The Casebook of Dr. Joel Hoffman

Arthur Porges

Edited by Richard Simms

Richard Simms Publications

This paperback first edition published in 2017

Richard Simms Publications, Surrey, England

ISBN: 978-0-9930387-2-3

The six stories collected in this volume first appeared in *Alfred Hitchcock's Mystery Magazine* from 1959 to 1963.

With special thanks to Cele Porges and Joel Hoffman. Thanks also to Mike Ashley for providing me with a copy of the story "Birds of One Feather."

For more information please visit The Arthur Porges Fan Site:

http://arthurporges.atwebpages.com

Contents

Introduction

The "locked room" or "impossible crime" story is a sub-genre in the world of mystery and detective literature with a long history and numerous revered past masters of the craft; John Dickson Carr, G. K. Chesterton and Arthur Conan Doyle are legendary names which readily come to mind.

As a young man, Arthur Porges read these authors avidly and once he had established himself as a full-time writer, he delighted in penning countless short stories within this disciplined literary form. Most of his contributions to the field featured various sleuths that appeared in more than one story. As well as Julian Morse Trowbridge, Ullyses Price Middlebie and Cyriack Skinner Grey, Porges' other main series detective was Dr. Joel Hoffman, a pathologist by profession who acts as consultant to Lieutenant Ader in investigating a number of particularly baffling crimes.

The Hoffman stories, of which there were six in total (and all assembled here for the first time in book form), were originally printed in issues of *Alfred Hitchcock's Mystery Magazine* from 1959 to 1963. Set on the California coast, these tales have a certain air of authenticity about them in terms of locale, and of course Porges' trademark attention to detail and meticulous plotting, for which he was renowned.

The stories involve murder mysteries, cunningly contrived and a challenge for Hoffman, who has a talent for thinking outside of the box, to solve. Porges invariably places the emphasis on the *how* element by which a homicide is carried out, as opposed to a straightforward whodunit—it is usually pretty obvious who the most likely suspect is in these stories. A scientific aspect often plays a part in providing a vital clue, the ingenious application of obscure facts from the realms of physics, chemistry or the natural world. The author's knowledge of ornithology, for example, features in more than one story, including my personal favorite "Circle in the Dust" which, ironically, is the only tale in this collection that does not feature a "locked room" mystery or "impossible crime."

Before I leave you to the stories themselves, a short word about the similarity between the plots of "No Killer Has Wings" and "A Puzzle in Sand." During my correspondence with the author, I remarked about this, to which Arthur replied that at the time both he and the editor were of course well aware of it, but with a knowing glee chose to repeat what was a brilliant premise, worthy of recycling! However, I should make clear here that the later story, "A Puzzle in Sand," is not a precise reworking of a scenario; both stories stand on their own as great reads.

And given the somewhat esoteric and rather abstruse knowledge called upon to solve the mysteries collected in this volume, if any reader can work out the solution to just one of these six cases before Dr. Joel Hoffman unravels the answer—then I take my hat off to them!

Richard Simms
Surrey, England
June, 2017

Dead Drunk

It takes a lot to stump an experienced pathologist, and even more to surprise him. Nor will any findings, no matter how grotesque, shock a man familiar with every use and abuse of the body.

But some weeks ago I was in at the finish of a case that made me dig deeper than is necessary in most of them, and had me tangled up in my own emotions like a kitten with a ball of yarn.

It was one of Lieutenant Ader's headaches. He and I have worked together, informally, for a number of years. Although I'm not officially connected with the Norfolk City Police, Pasteur Hospital is the only one around with a full-time pathologist on the staff. That's me—Dr. Joel Hoffman, middle-aged, unmarried—possibly because of my dedication to my work. And since the nearest adequate crime lab is a hundred and fifty miles away, Ader calls on me occasionally to carry out autopsies and other tests which the local coroner—a political hack—is unable to handle properly.

The case really began fifteen months ago, and oddly enough I was there, although without any idea of the ramifications to come later. At that time, the lieutenant was driving us back from a stabbing at the south end of town: a simple matter, with no subtleties, consisting of a steak knife driven into a lung. But on the way home, we heard a radio call about a traffic accident not too far off, and Ader decided to have a look. It never does any harm to barge in on your subordinates by surprise now and then; keeps them on their toes, Ader feels.

It turned out to be a typical and infuriating example of the genus legal murder. We found a huge garish convertible, a shaky driver, and a dazed woman crouching over the body of her child, a boy about eight.

As we pulled up, the man responsible for the tragedy was protesting to all and sundry, but especially to the pair of stony-faced officers from the prowl car.

"I'm not drunk," he insisted, his voice only slightly thick. "It's my diabetes; I need insulin. Sure, I had a couple, but I'm quite sober."

The man reeked of alcohol, but his actions were not those of a drunk. This is a familiar phenomenon. The shock of the accident had blasted the maggots from his nervous system, so that to the casual observer, he seemed in full command of himself.

I was busy with the child. There wasn't a hope. He died before the ambulance got there five minutes later. The mother, smartly dressed and attractive, knelt there pale and rigid, as if in a trance. It was that dangerous state before the blessed release of tears.

I never did learn the details of the accident. Apparently, mother and son, the latter leading a puppy, were waiting at the crosswalk, when the animal got away. Before the woman could stop him, the child had scampered into the street. He should have been safe in the crosswalk in any circumstances; the law is strict about that; but the car was moving too fast, and its driver was drunk. An old story.

Ader watched the interns put the pathetic little body into the ambulance. The heavy muscles of his jaw corded.

"I know this murderer and his convertible," Ader told me in a gritty voice. "He was sure to kill somebody sooner or later. A worthless guy if ever there was one. I wish we could nail him this time."

I took a good look at the man. Plump, expensively dressed, well tanned, sun-lamp style, not the kind you get out in the air. He had a jowly face with bags under the eyes. His earlier paleness was gone, but he seemed nervous, and yet arrogant, too, as if he anticipated a punch in the nose, and was ready to yell police brutality.

"You can't blame a man for diabetic coma, Lieutenant," he said defiantly. "You've tried it before, and the jury didn't buy any. I'm Gordon Vance Whitman, remember, not some scared, friendless punk you can frame."

"You're drunk," Ader said. "And you forgot the 'third' at the end of your distinguished name."

"Like hell I am. Diabetic coma." There was a sly glint in his small eyes.

I glanced at the lieutenant. He shrugged in disgust.

"We've had this guy up several times for drunk driving; nobody was killed before—just maimed. He has diabetes, all right; and the symptoms are rather similar, as you know. A jury isn't competent to assess the difference, not with a gaggle of high-priced lawyers working on them."

"The juries are fine," Whitman grinned, swaying a little. "All I need is a pill." With deliberate ostentation he pulled a vial from one pocket, opened it, and popped a tablet into his mouth. I spotted the label; the stuff was one of those new drugs which, for people over forty, takes the place of insulin. "Just a matter of excess blood sugar," he said, making sure the scene went on record.

"You don't seem much concerned about the child you killed," I told him, feeling a strong urge to mash a handful of knuckles against his beautifully capped teeth.

"Naturally, I'm very sorry," he replied in a solemn voice. "But it wasn't my fault; the kid ran out after that fool pup all of a sudden."

"That's no excuse," Ader snapped. "If you hadn't been soused and speeding, you could have stopped in plenty of time. You hit him in a crosswalk."

"If I *was* going too fast," Whitman explained, "it happened after the coma dazed me. I blanked out for a minute and may have stepped on the gas."

"You can at least see that he never drives again," I reminded Ader.

"Yeah," he said wearily. "That'll cheer the parents no end. You don't know the half of it, son. Let's get out of here: Briggs and Gerber can handle the details."

"Wait a minute," I said. "What about her?"

Ader jumped, as though startled. "You're right. I'm an idiot."

We both looked at the woman. She was still crouched there, but now she was cradling the puppy in her arms. A low, pathetic moaning came from her throat, and the little animal, tightly gripped and unhappy, joined in with a shrill whimper.

"Look," Ader said. "You and Briggs take her home in the cruiser. Get her husband, and call the family doctor."

It seemed a good idea. I managed to get her on her feet, and over to the police car. Briggs climbed in, and we were off. The low moaning became louder; suddenly she was weeping with passionate intensity. That was all to the good, though there are limits.

It's been at least ten years since I had a patient to treat. All of mine are just bodies to be studied. Nevertheless, I always carry a minimum emergency kit, and it came in handy now. I had a devil of a time, but finally managed to give her a sedative. I'll never forget that ride: the woman, her dainty dress all smeared from the gutter; her carefully made-up face a wild mask of grief; and that pitiful puppy's whimpering, incessant and at times shrill.

Twice the woman pulled away from me and tried to jump out of the moving car. "I want to go back!" she cried. "Where did they take Derry? Let me go; let me go!"

Well, we got her home at last, and called her husband, a college professor. He picked up the family doctor on the way, and I was relieved from duty. Briggs dropped me off at the hospital, where I found hours of work already piled up. Yet busy as I was, I couldn't get the incident off my mind. Do doctors ever get used to that sort of thing? I wondered. More than ever, I felt I'd been wise in avoiding general practice. It was too easy to get involved. For days I winced every time I thought of that poor woman and her loss.

Some time later, Ader gave me the whole sad story of Gordon Vance Whitman III. This character was a playboy of fifty plus and almost as many millions. One of the most sued people in the country. He'd never been any good, and the chief thing of interest about him was the foresight of his father, a canny old pirate of an earlier generation, when financial morals were even lower than now. He had put the boy's inheritance in the form of an unbreakable trust, of which Gordon enjoyed only the income. Such arrangements, which unfairly protect irresponsibles like Whitman against legitimate claims, are barred in most states, but not, alas, in mine. The income, of course, was enormous by ordinary standards, and cleverly designed to make tracing and attaching any portion of it as tricky as legally possible.

Whitman had married the usual series of showgirls, all of whom were collecting large slices of his assorted dividends; but other judgments, totaling millions, were unenforceable because of the machinations of the late Whitman, senior.

In short, Ader saw little hope of convicting Whitman this time either.

Well, I was too busy to keep track of one more social injustice—the needless death of a child—among many. I seem to recall that Whitman's license was revoked for a long time, and another large judgment added to the list. He beat the drunk charge, since blood tests are barred here. The old diabetes story was good again. As for transportation, there are chauffeurs available for a price, and after enough high-toned specialists had testified that his diabetes was under control, this model citizen may even have recovered his maiming rights.

Occasionally I saw an item about him—he was always news. Another marriage, a starlet this time. Apparently he favored petite redheads; this was the fourth to become Mrs. Whitman.

"A few more marriages," Ader remarked sourly once, "and maybe the guy'll be too worn out to drive around killing children!"

The accident happened over a year ago, and seemed to be past history, but last month saw a new phase of the Whitman story, and it was a lulu.

Ader phoned me late on a Tuesday afternoon. The body of a man had just been found inside a locked, third-floor apartment. No marks of violence; no sign of any other party's having been present, even. The victim had apparently enjoyed a lone binge behind a bolted door. He had then stretched out on the divan, and instead of awakening with a size-twelve head and lepidoptera in his stomach, never came to at all.

"And the dear departed," Ader told me with ghoulish satisfaction, "is none other than our old friend, Gordon Vance Whitman III."

"Good," I remarked. "But where do I fit in?"

"We have a curious policy here at headquarters. We'd like to know what this crumb died of."

"You'd better take the usual pictures, and then bring me the body," I told him. "I can't possibly leave the hospital today. In any case, it certainly sounds like a stroke or coronary."

"Very likely," Ader agreed. "But I have an instinct in these matters, and let's be sure, okay?"

"Fair enough. Bring me the remains, and I'll do the p.m. this evening."

At that stage, of course, there was no indication of murder, what with the locked door and all. There aren't many John Dickson Carr puzzles in real life.

The police brought me the body about five, and I got all the details and photos. It was a matter of luck that Whitman had been found so promptly. One of his numerous lady friends, unable to rouse him by leaning on the buzzer, had finally called the manager, who in turn notified the police. They had broken in, seen that the man was dead, and now it was up to me. We all expected that the cause of death was something quick, massive, and natural. I would have bet on it myself. Hence my first real surprise in years.

Now, an autopsy, when properly done, is a long and involved chore. The "gross" part, actually carried out on the table, is almost identical with a series of major operations, and performed with the same care and precision as if the person were still alive and under anaesthesia. No sloppy hacking will do; the job takes from three to six hours with a conscientious pathologist. The microscopic phase, completed in the laboratory, may go on for weeks, and could include work in chemistry, bacteriology, toxicology, and any other specialty you'd care to name.

My preliminary examination seemed to confirm the existence of some sort of respiratory failure, for the face was grey and the lips bluish—a condition called cyanosis. Nevertheless, there is a standard routine for a post mortem, so I began with the skull. The brain tissue was quite normal; no sign of a blood clot there, which ruled out one kind of stroke.

Next, working by the book, I explored the chest cavity, and found pay dirt immediately. The appearance of the lungs: the edema and signs of severe irritation, caught my eye at once. I bent over for a better look with a 3X magnifier, and as my face came close, noted an odd odor—the faint, musty smell of new-mown hay, along with the sharper, unmistakable reek of hydrochloric acid.

It was a clue I might easily have missed. That would have meant many hours of lab work to discover the obvious. You see, nobody who served in the Army would forget that scent of moldy hay. In the early months of 1942, when gas warfare seemed highly probable, every soldier, and particularly those of us in the Medical Corps, was taught to recognize the main types of poison gas. This unique smell meant phosgene, a deadly stuff invented during World War I. A few good whiffs, and the victim, beyond a little coughing and chest congestion, might go about his business unworried, only to collapse and die later, without warning. It's tricky and variable, forming hydrochloric acid in the lungs. Real nasty, that vapor.

I told you it was a puzzler—a man dead of phosgene in a locked room. The case was no longer one of death by natural causes or accident—not with the victim's lungs full of poison gas.

Now don't misunderstand me; I'm a pathologist, not a detective. Theoretically, when I completed the rest of the autopsy, my job was done. But when something this intriguing comes along, which is seldom, and they can spare me at the hospital, I like to tag along with the lieutenant. Sometimes I've been helpful; at worst, I'm a useful sounding board.

Well, he took me to the apartment, where I got another jolt. I'd assumed, reasonably enough, that somebody had pumped phosgene into the room; there didn't seem to be any other explanation. But I was wrong. A few simple tests showed that no such wholesale release of gas had occurred. Fantastic as it seemed, the stuff must have been introduced directly into the man's lungs—and only there. That seemed to imply a tank of phosgene, along with a tube or mask. It was a sticker, all right.

But Ader skipped that point for the moment. Instead we concentrated on the source, thinking that would be easier. You don't just pick up a tank of war gas at the corner drugstore. It's not too hard to make a little of it, chemically, but not in any form that would permit it being pumped into a person's lungs.

The lieutenant checked all the nearby Army camps. We weren't too surprised to find that none of them stocked the stuff. Gas warfare is nearly passé. All they had were those recognition kits which teach rookies the characteristic odors. Harmless samples. The one big chemical-warfare depot was able to state positively that no phosgene—stored in big tanks—was missing.

That left the question of motive, which gave us both a grim chuckle. It was obvious that Gordon Vance Whitman III had plenty of enemies. Not so many as the late Hitler, maybe, but quite a few.

The money angle was a flop. Whitman had no heirs. In the event of his death, the huge trust became a sort of foundation like the Ford or Rockefeller setup. Which meant that none of those judgments would be any better than they were now—in short, useless to the litigants.

Well, police work is mostly tiresome routine. Somebody had murdered, and how we still didn't know, the late Mr. Whitman. Therefore it was a matter of motive. Ader and his staff had to check out a list of more than twenty prime suspects, all people with good reasons for hating the victim. I withdrew from that part of the case; they were yelling for me at the hospital anyway. Instead, I continued to ponder the phosgene problem. I kept gnawing at it during the weeks Ader's crew was struggling with the legwork.

Their efforts finally paid off. Everybody was eliminated from the list, but one woman. She was definitely It. Oddly enough, the lieutenant hadn't felt strongly about including her at the start; it was almost certain, he thought, that she had no connection with the case. But the principles of sound police work sink deep into a competent officer, and her name was added to the others. You see, she was merely the maid who cleaned the hallways and did similar odd jobs. The apartments themselves were the problem of the tenants.

She called herself Mrs. Talbot, but the first thorough check soon revealed that her right name was Eleanor Oldenburger. A college graduate, the widow of a distinguished professor, she had recently suffered a complete nervous collapse. She had taken this job a few weeks after leaving the hospital. On the off chance that her arriving at this particular building might be significant, Ader looked for a connection between Whitman and her. It didn't take long to find one.

If anybody had a good reason to loathe the late playboy, Mrs. Oldenburger qualified in spades. We were brought back fifteen months to the killing of that little boy. His name was Derry, and he was the Oldenburger's only child. Loss of the boy had undoubtedly hastened the professor's death. Their small amount of insurance went for the widow's medical expenses—nervous breakdowns come high. A damage suit initiated by the professor before his death had resulted in a judgment of $300,000, but there were dozens of others ahead of it, all uncollectible.

When Ader told me all this, I looked him in the eye, and said, "If she did kill him, more power to her. Why not drop the case now?"

He didn't lower his own stare for a moment.

"I'm a police officer. I can't do that. I'm no judge; you know that." A crooked little smile touched his lips. "I certainly want to know *how* she managed it, but if there isn't enough evidence to make a case, I won't be heartbroken." He paused. "Husband, child—all lost because of that stinker. You can't really blame her."

"What's she like?" I asked him.

"You saw her. Woman in her forties, I'd say. So far, I've seen her only at work, not in her home, in those shapeless things maids wear for dirty jobs. I've a hunch it was mostly protective coloration. I seem to remember a pair of electric-blue eyes that didn't fit a common drudge at all. But I'm about to visit her at home. Why not come along?"

I jumped at the chance. Although I was no nearer to a solution of the phosgene puzzle, the woman began to interest me for herself. Whatever her plan, it showed a cool, keen intelligence, as well as the ruthless judgment of a Minerva.

She lived in a tiny but immaculate apartment in Orange Grove. I saw Ader blink at the sight of her. She wore well-tailored slacks of grey material, and a pale-blue blouse; they emphasized a slender, but rounded figure that suggested twenty-five rather than forty-five. Her hair was of the sort Holmes called "positive blonde," that is, fair, but with highlights and subtle colors. She seemed quite relaxed.

With almost insolent coolness, she insisted on our having martinis. When we were settled with ours, she curled up catlike on a big sofa and gave us a faint smile.

"Let the inquisition begin," she said lightly. On the surface she was hard, cold, and callous. As a doctor, trained to study people behind their pathetic façades, I knew that her nerves were stretched to an unbearable tension, that she was on the knife-edge of hysteria.

Ader was brusque. I think he too sensed her delicate balance and hoped to break her down.

"Why didn't you tell us your real name?"

Her smile deepened.

"Come, Lieutenant. I was taking a menial job, under very distressing circumstances. Why should I parade my identity as a fallen woman?"

"You deliberately picked that building to work in. The manager testified that you phoned her repeatedly. Why did it have to be there? Wasn't it so you could get at Whitman?"

"You know, of course," she reminded him sweetly, "that I needn't answer any of these questions without a lawyer. But I've nothing to hide. I liked the location; as you see, it's near this apartment. I could walk; I'm too nervous these days to drive, and can't afford a car, anyway. And what makes you think I'd want to kill Whitman?"

"Look, Mrs. Oldenburger," Ader said. "We know about Derry. In case you've forgotten, Dr. Hoffman and I happened to be on the spot just after that swine, Whitman—"

She was deathly pale now, but interrupted him in an even voice.

"You agree, then, that he was a swine."

"Of course. I sympathize with you in every way. But I can't condone murder."

"Neither can you prove it," she flashed. "I understand his apartment was bolted inside."

"The transom was partly open. Isn't it true that you use a small ladder to clean woodwork in the halls?"

"Yes. I'm only five feet six, you see."

"Were you using it that day?"

"Yes. Did I crawl through the transom and kill Whitman?"

Ader frowned. "No, it's too small even for you. I measured it."

She gave him a look of mock consternation. "Oh, dear. And me bragging about my slender build."

"We don't know how you did it—yet. But obviously you found out where he lived, and wangled this job as a maid. Somehow you managed to fill his lungs with poison gas—phosgene, to be exact. It's only a matter of time before we discover the method."

She raised her carefully penciled brows, and squirmed deeper into the soft cushions. She seemed perfectly relaxed, but I could see a significantly throbbing vein by one ear.

"Phosgene? I doubt if I could spell it, in spite of my general chemistry in college. As for that job, I had a complete breakdown. Probably you know all about that, too. For weeks I was catatonic. When I recovered, any mental effort was still impossible. I had to find some simple physical work. That's all there is to it. I'm no scientific genius to make poison gas and get it into a locked room."

"What makes you think it had to be made?" Ader snapped. "Why not bought?"

She tightened visibly, aware of her mistake.

"Can you go out and buy poison gas?" she asked brightly. "I wouldn't know. But, in any case, gentlemen, it's getting late, and if you don't mind ..."

We left then; there wasn't much else to do. She was under a terrific strain, but wouldn't crack. Yet I felt sure reaction and regrets were inevitable. And I didn't like the prospect.

But intellectual curiosity is a passion with me, so I couldn't quit. And the next day I made my first real advance. I placed the name Oldenburger. Surely I had seen some of his articles in the past. What had they covered? Then it came to me; the man had been a top physiological chemist, often consulted by the big poison centers.

I got in touch with the nearest one immediately, with highly significant results. The puzzle was solved now, except for one small item. Ader supplied that, but didn't know it. It was the first time I held out on him. I merely asked for a list of cleaning agents available to the maids in Whitman's building. Among them, sure enough, was carbon tetrachloride, kept on hand to remove spots from upholstery. I decided to pay Mrs. Oldenburger a visit on my own.

This time she wore a simple dress, the kind that is tasteful-expensive-simple, if you know what I mean. It confirmed my suspicion that she was far from broke, and didn't actually need a job as maid.

Seeing her again, I realized what an attractive woman she really was. Without Ader there, she seemed to be more natural. As I'd suspected, the hardness and diamond sparkle had been at least partially assumed before—a shield.

My emotions were clawing me. I meant to prove I knew the solution, but after that—well, the way wasn't clear at all.

I accepted a drink, and for some minutes we made small talk. I began to lose hope of getting through, because the woman was at peace with herself. Apparently her conscience had been stilled; perhaps she had finally rationalized the murder to the point of feeling no guilt.

Relaxed and warm, she had that rare facility of withholding the best part of her considerable beauty, and then in a dazzling stroke, flashing it like a weapon. I had no defense against it and didn't seem to want one.

The small talk had to end sometime. I took the plunge.

"I know exactly how you did it," I told her.

A slight shadow passed over her face.

"I was more afraid of you than of the officer," she said. "My husband mentioned your work occasionally. A new test for morphine poisoning, I believe."

I may have blushed; this was, naturally, hardly what I expected as a counter.

"Thank you. And I know about Professor Oldenburger. He had a very intriguing case once at the poison center. Maybe he discussed it with you. Whitman's addiction to liquor was the key. It's an odd fact of chemistry that if a man with plenty of alcohol in his system gets a few whiffs of carbon tetrachloride, the two compounds unite in the blood to form phosgene, one of the deadliest of the early war gases. Now I believe you soaked a rag in the spot remover, and using a mop handle or something, reached through the transom to hold the cloth over Whitman's nose and mouth. With the ladder it was a cinch. Two or three minutes would be enough time. If anybody had appeared, you could have pulled away from the transom and busied yourself with the moldings. Besides, who knows better than a maid how deserted those apartments are by day?" I looked at her pale, composed face. "Am I right? There are no witnesses here, so why not admit it?"

She sat there, a fragile figure, with that odd air of repose, and my heart went out to her.

"Not quite," she said shakily. "I used a fishing rod. Rufus—my husband—was a great one for trout. It was the rod," she added, with a catch in her voice, "he taught Derry on." She turned her head away for a moment.

"It's hardly a case to stand up in court," I told her. "I doubt if any jury—"

"No," she said passionately. "You mustn't say that. I've been mad, distracted. It was a terrible thing. I have nightmares when I think of putting that awful rag—a sleeping man, helpless ..." She straightened in the chair. "I've signed a confession. I want you to call Lieutenant Ader."

To my surprise, I found myself protesting. The words came in a wild flood. I told her without my testimony, there was no case; that I wouldn't go to court. That Ader didn't know about the spot remover. She smiled as if I were a child.

She pled guilty, but by law a trial is still possible. I got the best lawyer in the state. I was now convinced she had been temporarily insane, and that was the line we held. The jury wouldn't convict.

During the long weeks of legal maneuvering, we grew closer together. I never dreamed I'd marry a murderess, but, as I said at the start, it's not easy to shock a pathologist.

Horse-Collar Homicide

I've been on some rather unusual cases with Lieutenant Ader. As the only qualified pathologist in the area, I help out the Norfolk Police occasionally, since they don't trust their coroner, a political hack. You might say I'm an unofficial crime lab—that's me, Dr. Joel Hoffman.

Now of all the fantastic homicides we've tackled together, the weirdest in a long time is the one I think of as "the man who died grinning through a horse-collar." That description has a kind of insane rhythm to it that appeals to me.

The case began with the mysterious death of Leonard Bugg Lakewood, head of one of the older Norfolk families.

I was examining some tissue under the microscope, when Lt. Ader popped into Pasteur Hospital to ask my advice.

"This is a real tricky one, Joel," he said. "Looks like natural death—a stroke—but the family doctor is none too sure, and I don't like the overall smell of the situation. Thought I'd kick it around with you before insisting on an autopsy."

I sighed. In ninety-nine per cent of such cases, it turns out to be by natural causes, but only after weary hours of lab work eliminating the abnormal. Still, the public should be grateful to people like Ader, who don't automatically take the easy way out. Besides, he does have a remarkably good nose for the scent of murder.

"Okay," I said. "Fill me in on the big picture, and we'll go on from there."

In such matters Ader is very concise, as if giving testimony; you could write down a very neat outline by recording his words verbatim. It seems that Lakewood, a man of sixty-three, was a sort of benevolent—well, maybe not so benevolent, either—tyrant. He was strong for tradition, and proud of his English ancestry, which goes back to William the Conqueror. The way he told it—often and loud—Lakewoods fought for Charles I, smuggled aristocrats out of revolutionary France, and died with the Light Brigade. Not the same ancestor, of course.

At least once a year, either at Christmas or on some anniversary of a Lakewood historical triumph, he gave a family party in the old style—the kind of affair you find in "Pickwick" or Irving's "Bracebridge Hall." It tickled the man to revive ancient diversions and bully his long-suffering relatives into participating for prizes.

"There's your motive," I said airily. "Anybody could get killed for such a foul scheme. Did he set up a maypole in the patio?"

"Think you're exaggerating?" Ader grunted. "They've had some fine 18th Century May Day celebrations on the grounds. But this time it was just a run of the mill affair, with only the immediate family present. The latest gimmick in old games was the rural sport of grinning through a horse-collar."

"Did you say 'grinning'? And through a horse-collar?" I asked.

"That's right. They were celebrating some Lakewood who shot a Cromwell general in the rump. The way this game is played, you hang up a horse-collar. Then each person gets behind it and makes funny faces with his head framed in the thing. The one who gets the most yaks wins."

"On that basis, Red Skelton could have been King of England. What does he win—a horse to fit the collar?"

"In this case," Ader said sourly, "the prize seemed to be a fatal stroke. The old man performed last. He had just stuck his head inside, and was mugging like crazy, when kaboom—he has a kind of epileptic fit, and falls down deader than a salted mackerel. Now I ask you!"

"What's to ask? The man was over sixty, after all. Too much excitement. Any previous evidence of epilepsy?"

"That's the point—none. The old boy was healthy as a stud bull. The only time he'd ever been inside a hospital was during the First World War. He was wounded."

"Just for the record, then, who would want to kill him?"

"Anybody in the family, the way I see it."

"You have a rather jaundiced view. Do all parents seem likely murder victims to the Norfolk Police?"

"There's more of that tendency in the average family than most people realize," Ader said soberly. "Parents hang on too tightly in this country."

"Don't let's get Freudian," I begged. "Who's in this homicidal family of Lakewood's?"

"I'll tell you," Ader said. "His second wife, Ethel—she's about forty-five. Two sons: Walter, aged thirty-four, and James, thirty-one—both by his first wife. Then there's a daughter of his and Ethel's—Jeanette. She's twenty-three."

"What became of his first wife?"

"She couldn't take it. Divorced him soon after James was born. Probably she named Queen Victoria as correspondent!"

"Both boys married, I presume."

"Oh, no," Ader snapped. "Single, and not enjoying their freedom one bit."

I raised my brows at this, and he said: "There's a good motive, all right. Way I hear it, the old man kept the family under his thumb financially; and even when the sons managed to meet young women, they were never up to Papa's standards for the Lakewoods. When you add to that the distribution of close to a million bucks in stocks and bonds ... It's a screwy situation all right. The boys were never allowed to work for a living. Mentally, their father was back in the 18th Century, when gentlemen didn't do anything commercial."

"Then how did he accumulate a million dollars?"

"Ah, it's all right to inherit money. *His* father was a tycoon—oil, I think."

"So the boys just sat around playing gentlemen."

"Not quite—that's the hell of it. There was too much Victorian Century. They couldn't work, but they had to study Greek and Latin. And the diversions of a gentleman—wine, women and gambling—were taboo. They went to college, but only for classics, although both boys managed to sneak in a few science courses. James tried chemistry, and Walter physics; but Lakewood found out, so they didn't get very far. As for Jeanette, the old man didn't know it, but she was studying shorthand and typing on the sly, and would have escaped at any moment. Still, there was no open rebellion by anybody."

"Brother," I said. "I see what you mean about motive. But still, on the surface, it sounds more like natural death. Why are you in doubt?"

He shrugged.

"Partly instinct; partly the family doctor. He says that the attack was almost a classic of the epileptic type, and yet there's no previous history of epilepsy. He feels that a fatal bout without any earlier warnings is very uncommon. Also there was some monkey business with the lights."

"Such as?"

"When Lakewood was making funny faces through the horse-collar, the lights flickered briefly just before he had that stroke."

"You're thinking of electrocution?"

"At first I did. But I don't need an expert to rule that out. The man had a normal heart. A slight jolt wouldn't do it; and there are no burns left by a strong current. It's mighty hard to electrocute a healthy man on a dry floor. You need very good contacts and high voltage for several seconds. He never even touched the horse-collar to any extent; and the whole family was in the room, far out of reach."

"What got you into the case officially?"

"The doctor. He's reluctant to sign a death certificate without a post mortem. A good man."

"Must be Dr. Lewis; he's the only first class diagnostician around."

"You guessed it."

"Well," I reminded him, "it's up to you. You have the legal right to demand an autopsy."

"I know," he said unhappily. "But if I'm wrong, the D.A. will crucify me, let alone the family."

"Nevertheless, you want one." I know Ader. He'd drag the devil out of Hell by the tail on Friday the 13th if there was an official subpoena for Old Nick.

"I've no choice, seeing that Lewis feels the way he does. The body will be brought here tonight. Give it the works, will you?"

"It just came to me," I grinned. "The obvious cause of death." I paused, and Ader brightened. "Horse-cholera!"

"Fun-nee!" Ader growled. "Remember—I want your super-special p.m. on the corpse."

"Roger and out. Now let me get back to my cancer cells."

The next day I did the autopsy on Lakewood. Following the usual routine, I started with the skull. It wasn't much use to look further. My first find was a surprise indeed: the old man had a metal plate in his head, one of those platinum jobs they used in World War I. Apparently, he'd suffered a nasty skull injury, probably from a shell fragment, and needed the plate to protect the brain until there was a fresh growth of bone. Over the years, new bone had covered the metal quite nicely, so that the outside of his head was as good as ever. Now platinum is one of the noble elements, and doesn't corrode easily. After forty years or so, this thin patch, however, was somewhat darkened and discolored, which seemed a little strange. Still, I was more intrigued by the brain tissue around the platinum. It was a mess. I couldn't make much sense out of the situation. It was not a stroke caused by the usual broken blood vessel; the damage was too extensive and abnormal for that. The brain tissue looked more as if acid had been injected, or a hot poker mashed around. Yet there wasn't so much as a hair out of place on the outside. If a needle, or heat, or electricity had reached the brain, it didn't go through the scalp and bone. This was a real baffler.

I went through the rest of the p.m., but didn't expect to find anything else, and wasn't disappointed. Of course, the microscopic and chemical tests remained, and could take weeks, but they seemed uncalled for. Lakewood had undoubtedly died because of deep, widespread brain lesions, and those alone. Yet it looked as if Ader and Lewis were right to be suspicious, since nowhere in the literature could I find any natural cause that would explain the injuries.

I reported all this to the lieutenant, and it didn't make him happy.

"I appreciate your information, Joel, but unless we know the 'how and why' of this mysterious damage, we can't even begin to build a case. We still don't know it's even murder. There could be a natural cause—some crazy accident, or a new type of disease."

"That's possible, but highly unlikely. In any case, I'd know a little more if I could get the complete details of the party. Are you planning to question the family again?"

"I'll have to. I got only the main facts last time. So if you'd like to come along ..."

"You bet I would."

He arranged to pick me up the next morning, and left. I devoted some concentrated thought to the problem overnight, but got nowhere slowly. They say you can't poison an egg without getting through the shell, which is sure to give it away. That seemed to be one phase of the problem here. If Lakewood was murdered, the killer got to his brain without piercing scalp or skull. Furthermore, he—or she—did it without being near the victim. On the surface that was so far-fetched a theory that I began to think maybe Ader was right, and we were up against a new disease. I was still brooding about it when I dozed off late that night.

The following morning Ader came by at nine, and we went out to the Lakewood house, a huge quasi-Greek mansion with extensive grounds. We got the family together and grilled them. They were resentful, but passive; the old man had apparently knocked all the fight out of them, which made our job easier. I studied them, while they were being examined by Ader, as if hoping to spot a possible murderer by inspection.

Ethel Lakewood was a faded, twittery woman who suggested a dancing mouse. As a killer, she hardly seemed to qualify, except that I know better. There are no obvious characteristics that typify a murderer.

Walter, the older son, was a thin, nervous type, with hot, intolerant eyes. He had thick, spiky hair that made him resemble one of those Bolshevik bombers so popular with cartoonists a generation ago. His voice was startlingly deep, as if belonging to a much larger frame.

The other son, James, was still trying to play Joe College. Perhaps he felt that the old man had wasted his children's youth, and he wanted to hang on to what was left of his. But a balding man of thirty-one, with plenty of jowl, can't look much like a sophomore.

The only refreshing sight among this bunch was Jeanette, a slim, dark girl, almost Italianate in appearance, with a yummy figure and eyes that danced with vivacity. Evidently Lakewood had not yet succeeded in crushing her spirit, and I couldn't help rejoicing that now he never would.

Since James was the most articulate, Ader let him do practically all the talking. He brought out the horse-collar, and showed us how it had been suspended in the doorway of the huge parlor. The long hall behind it was kept dark, so that in the blaze of the brilliantly lit room each face framed by the collar was sharply etched, and every grimace visible to the audience.

I studied the heavy thing as James babbled. He was delighted to mingle with us commoners, having been starved for companionship, it would seem. The collar suggested a giant's toilet seat to my inexperienced eye but then I'm unfamiliar with draft horses, although I risk a buck or two on the racing kind occasionally.

"Now tell me," Ader was saying, "was this thing just hung up in the doorway, or was there more to it?"

"It was fastened right there," James said. "Naturally it was braced so as not to swing around, and it was decorated too. All sorts of colored paper around it. Walter fixed it up that way. Father wasn't sure that was right, but Walter read it in a book."

"He didn't know as much about old customs as he thought," Walter rumbled in that incongruous bass of his.

James tittered. "He was flabbergasted that you actually looked up anything," he said. "Usually you didn't care any more than we did. All of us wanted to get the fool party over, and didn't care one bit how accurate the games were. We always let Father win, anyhow. It made him easier to get along with."

"Now, boys," their mother twittered. "You know it was really very charming."

"You needn't pretend, Mother," Jeanette said firmly. "You hated it as much as we did. People have to live in the present. Daddy was mentally disturbed—why not admit it?"

"Why, Jeanette—I never—" The little woman suggested an agitated parakeet in her flutterings.

"What about the lights?" Ader cut in. "I understand they flickered in a peculiar way."

"That's right," James said eagerly, anxious to regain the floor. "You remember, Ma—Father was just making those funny faces, pulling out the corners of his mouth with his fingers, when the lights dimmed and brightened again. He sort of reeled back, with a crazy, wild look, clapped his hands to his head, and then tumbled forward. He rolled right under the horse-collar into this room, and when we ran over, he was dead."

"How's the wiring here?" Ader demanded. "Any overload?"

"Oh, my, no," Mrs. Lakewood said. "What with electric ovens and air conditioners and washer-driers, we had special cables put in, didn't we, boys?"

"That's true," James said. "No reason for our lights to flicker. Must have been something at the power-house." He gave that thin giggle again. "Maybe a sparrow on the wire outside. Walter would know— he's the physics expert around here."

"Some expert," his brother boomed. "I had just two lousy semesters when the old man butted in."

"Daddy wanted him to study Greek and Latin," Jeanette added. "He said that's all a gentleman needed. Dead languages. And for me, music, embroidery—ugh!"

"Now, Jeanette!" her mother protested.

"Did anybody leave the room," Ader asked, "while Mr. Lakewood was performing?"

They looked at each other.

"Mother was here, and Jeanie," James said. "And Walter—he was in the armchair."

"That's right," Walter agreed. "We were all here. Nobody would have dared to leave while Father was doing his stuff."

That seemed to be all Ader could think of, so he broke up the conference. He took the horse-collar along, since it was the only evidence we were likely to have. Neither of us felt very hopeful about it. I think he brought it because there was nothing else available. Even then, he passed the buck to me.

"If the old guy was murdered," he growled, "this may have been involved—don't ask me how. I wish you'd take it to your lab and go over it."

"Right," I said. "I'll have another go at the skull, too. I'm far from satisfied with what we've got so far. Maybe I missed the boat."

"More like a submarine," he said.

No doubt about it, Ader was unhappy. If after taking the body away from the family and messing it about, we came up with a fat nothing, the D.A. would singe his tail good.

That afternoon I put the horse-collar on a table, and scrutinized it with minute care. The staff had a good laugh at my expense. I won't repeat the comments about horse-doctor Hoffman, and did the patient die of the heaves.

The collar was made of wood covered with leather, and a faint odor of the stable still clung to it. There were a number of tiny studs, or nails, forming a pleasing pattern, and, on the whole, it had the good proportions that go with something that's functional. At a certain angle I could see striations, as if something had been wound about the collar in tight strands, but assumed they were marks of the decorative padding.

Getting exactly nowhere with the horse-collar, I decided to have another look at Lakewood's head. This time, as I twisted and pried, studying scalp and bone, something hit the table-top with a tiny click. I picked it up, and found to my surprise that it was a silver filling.

I had made a casual examination of the old man's dentition, noting that he was one of the lucky few who retain most of their teeth through the age of sixty. Now I went over his mouth again. The silver filling was the only metal one, although there were a few plastic jackets. I wondered why this plug was loose enough to drop out. Was it just a coincidence? I couldn't help thinking there was some simple tie-in eluding me in a tantalizing way.

My real break came just a few minutes later. I went back to the horse-collar to put it away. But when I picked it up, I noticed that a stray paper clip was sticking strangely to one place on the leather. I pulled it off, and there were nail-heads underneath. I touched the clip to the pattern at other points, and it clung. The clip itself wasn't magnetized, I found; therefore the nails were. How did they get that way?

Now, although I called myself jokingly a one-man crime lab, I'm primarily a pathologist. I don't know beans about electricity and magnetism, and would rather dissect an elephant than tinker with my wife's vacuum cleaner. But like any scientifically trained man, I can locate information. In this case, I used the brain picking technique. In short, I paid a visit to Professor Harry Matison, who teaches physics at the Norfolk Institute of Technology. What he told me tore the case wide open.

In order for those nails to become magnetized, they would have to be rubbed one by one with a magnet, which is hardly practicable—*or* the collar would have to be exposed to a strong magnetic field. This last meant either passing the collar through a charged coil, or, more likely, winding wires about the leather to make the whole thing itself into one huge coil.

"All right," I asked Harry, my excitement growing, "suppose this horse-collar was wire-wound, and had current passing through it—would that electrocute a man who put his head inside?"

"Electrocute! No, no, no—you could keep your noggin there all day. But just hold a piece of metal in your hand—a good conductor, like steel or aluminum—inside the coil, and it'll be white hot in seconds. That is," he added hastily, "if you've enough windings and the right amperage. But only metals are affected that way. They melt ores in a vacuum by such induced currents—no wires need touch the metal."

"Suppose the man had a platinum plate in his skull."

He whistled softly.

"You're the pathologist. Suppose the plate got even red-hot for half a second—and it could very easily. What would that do to the brain?"

"I know what it did," I said grimly. "And would it also affect metal fillings in the teeth—say expand and loosen them?"

"Why," he said, "you'd put your head through the ceiling. Imagine a white-hot filling against a nerve!"

Well, that put the lid on it. Ader's men found tiny bits of wire in Walter's room—he was the frustrated physicist, remember. It was easy enough to trace purchase of several hundred feet of wire to him. He had volunteered to prepare the horse-collar, and even invented an authority for covering the thing with tinsel, so as to hide the windings. He knew about the old man's war-wound; the younger children and second wife apparently had forgotten if they were ever told. It was a simple matter to bring a lead and switch under the rug to his favorite armchair. Then, when Lakewood's head was nicely framed in what was then a powerful electric coil, Walter just reached behind the seat to complete a momentary connection. The metal plate must have been red-hot almost instantly, and the result very much like fatal epilepsy.

Confronted with all these facts, Walter broke down, and confessed. If he'd bluffed it out, we might have had our troubles in court, so fantastic was the truth. But his father had softened the boy's spine, and there would never be any fight in him. At the sentencing, he acted so peculiarly that they sent him to an institution instead of the chair. I'm not sure he wasn't better off there than at home under the old man's regime.

The house was sold; Mrs. Lakewood left town, and Jeanette soon got a good job as secretary to the President of Star Records.

I was most pleased with James, however. He married a red-headed showgirl, and promises to run through his third of a million in record time.

Circle in the Dust

It isn't often that Lieutenant Ader brings me a simple murder involving the traditional blunt instrument. For that kind, even the political hack of a coroner is good enough. Ader keeps me in reserve for the tricky ones, since I'm the only qualified pathologist in these parts—Joel Hoffman, officially on the staff of Pasteur Hospital, but more informally, and through friendship, the lieutenant's one-man crime lab.

In this latest case the cause of death was quite obvious—no hidden subtleties at all. Nothing like the Whitman affair with its locked door and phosgene gas, or the Lakewood murder with that crazy horse-collar gimmick.

This time we had a harmless old lady killed with one blow from a heavy object. There was no possibility of her having been hit by mistake; somebody had taken a single powerful swing with intent to murder. One side of the victim's skull was badly crushed; death must have been instantaneous.

"It's the motive that makes things rough on this one," Ader told me when I'd finished the autopsy. "Here's an old woman who'd never harmed a soul. All right, that wouldn't matter; some characters will kill a saint for sixty-nine cents, but she didn't have any money. There's no possible doubt about that. She was living on a small annuity which was to lapse at her death. Less than $200 in her bank account, and a mortgaged house full of trashy furniture and whatnots. I don't get it."

"Maybe whoever killed her thought she had money stashed away," I suggested. "Most old people living alone are always suspected of being secret misers."

"That doesn't seem to figure. If a stranger killed her hoping to find dough, he'd have ransacked the house. Well, nothing was touched. Probably she admitted the killer herself, which doesn't prove much, since they tell me the old woman was so trusting as to be almost simple minded."

"Low I.Q.," I said. "Like that other innocent one, called Jesus."

"You know what I mean," he snapped. Ader hates irony.

"Apology accepted. It's just that I get tired of hearing people called idiots because they don't invariably expect the worst from their fellow men."

"Don't go philosophical on me," Ader said sourly. "I don't remember Plato breaking any tough cases."

"Any fingerprints in the place?"

"Everybody's. At least those who were there in the last five years. The old gal wasn't much of a housekeeper."

"Tell me about her," I suggested. "So far you haven't given me anything to hang one of my fantastic theories on."

"There isn't much to tell. She was a widow—a Mrs. Valerie Antoine. Came to California from New England. Bought a little wooden house here in Norfolk. Picked it, I'd guess, because her nephew lives in town. Everybody liked her—a harmless, motherly old woman of sixty-five."

"Who profits by her death?"

"That's the hell of it; there simply isn't any profit. I've checked up on her possessions. The nephew, Ray Zittenfield, inherits, but all he'll get is the mortgaged house, full of junk, and whatever is left of her two hundred bucks in the bank after burial expenses. Nobody would kill a chicken without a better motive than that." He paused. "Unless she saw something that somebody couldn't risk having her report."

"Not very likely," I told him. "If you read the autopsy report, you'll remember she had cataracts on both eyes. She wouldn't have been able to tell Elsa Maxwell from a Singer midget at ten paces. Maybe we'd better look for a pathological killer with no connection—somebody who picked her because she was handy."

"Not on your life," Ader retorted. "That's all right for a last resort. Right now it's premature."

"Then what do you suggest, Maestro?"

"I expect you to do the suggesting," he said coolly. "But first how about going over to her house with me? Maybe you'll spot something we didn't."

"Anybody there? Besides the inevitable Sergeant Briggs, I mean?"

"The nephew. He's staying in the house until things are cleared up."

"Hope it's not a life sentence," I murmured, and Ader glared at me. He doesn't appreciate levity during a case.

We drove out to the scene of the crime, a small wooden building at least thirty years old. A decade ago you could buy such a place for $5000, and there were few enough customers. Now, what with every American determined to acquire his own mortgage, plus the inflation, a shack like this costs $10,000. That was a possible angle, I thought; maybe the nephew hoped to sell the place at a profit.

After seeing and talking to him, however, I had my doubts. There are no obvious traits that identify a murderer, but Zittenfield certainly didn't seem to have the nerve and ruthlessness to kill a fragile old lady in cold blood. He was a nervous, pale young man, who talked so fast he tended to stutter. His glasses were so powerful, they made his blue eyes look like some rare species of fish in thick glass bowls.

He led us on a tour of the house. The lower floor was sparsely furnished; after all, how much does one old lady need? But the upper floor, which was really nothing but an attic consisting of one large room, told another story. There was a junk heap, if I ever saw one. Every foot was piled high with trash: old furniture, crayon portraits of long-dead great aunts, hideous Victorian nymphs holding grapes of green glass, and several tons of similar rubbish.

"Any of this stuff valuable?" I asked the nephew. "Is it possible she has some offbeat treasures here that some sharpie wanted badly enough to kill her?"

He looked a bit unhappy, and Ader gave him a sharp glance.

"Nothing that I know of," he said, "except a scrimshaw work—that might bring a few hundred dollars. I urged her to sell it, but she wouldn't listen to me."

"What's scrimshaw work?" Ader demanded. "And where is it now?"

"Over here. I knew better than to touch anything until you police gave the word. That sergeant outside warned me, too." He led us to a small wooden chest perched on top of a moth-eaten red sofa. When he raised the lid, we saw a fantastic collection of intricately carved doodads. There were letter openers, pie-crimpers, and even back-scratchers, mostly white, but with a few black items.

"Made from whale teeth, shark-jaws, and the like," the boy explained. "Aunt Val's great-grandfather was a New Bedford whaling captain. Jared Gray, related to Asa Gray, the famous botanist. Captain Gray left all this junk to his son, who left it to his, and so on down to my aunt. Except for the scrimshaw it's awful trash, but she wouldn't consider selling or giving any of it away. She hero-worshipped the old boy, I guess. She was easygoing about everything else, but just try to separate her from anything of the captain's, and no mule could have been more stubborn."

"And you wanted her to peddle these whale-tooth carvings?"

"Naturally. It was the only valuable stuff he left her. It wasn't doing her any good up here. If she got three or four hundred dollars, she could do some of the things she'd always wanted to. Like fixing up the place a bit; the termites are eating three meals a day here. I know a dealer—" He broke off, as if afraid of having said too much.

"I suppose you had a little commission in mind," the lieutenant said pleasantly.

The boy flushed.

"Well, it was my idea," he said. "She didn't know it was worth anything. But if even one piece disappeared she'd know that in a hurry. I wouldn't have made more than fifty bucks on the whole deal."

It was easy to read between the lines. He'd tried removing one of the better pieces to see if she'd spot the theft. Obviously, she had noticed it.

"We'll have this stuff priced by an expert," Ader said.

I knew what he was thinking. Suppose those bone carvings were worth thousands? That would give Mr. Zittenfield a real motive.

"I'm telling the truth," the old lady's nephew insisted. "That stuff won't bring more than $300. Of course, the dealer will get at least a thousand, but that's the antique business for you. Tremendous mark-up."

Meanwhile, I prowled the rest of the room, squinting in the glaring afternoon sun that beat on one wall from the big, dusty windows. Suddenly I gave a low whistle, and Ader was at my side in one tigerish bound. He saw what I did, and no words were necessary. In the middle of a dust-covered table near the wall was a round mark suspiciously clean. Undoubtedly some object with a circular base had recently stood there. Ader called the nephew over.

"What was on this table?" he demanded.

The boy looked blank.

"I can't remember," he said, frowning. "All I ever paid much attention to was the scrimshaw. The rest isn't worth anything. Believe me, I know, Lieutenant. I've been interested in antiques for several years. Take my word for it, the rest of this tripe wouldn't bring twenty-five dollars."

"Yeah?" Ader sounded sceptical. "Somebody carried off whatever stood on this table. There must be a reason. Try to remember what your aunt kept there."

"I'm trying," Zittenfield said. "But who could keep track of all this junk? I was only here two or three times, and my last visit was over a year ago. You tell me what was in your aunt's house last time you were there."

Ader looked sheepish. He'd been too busy this year even to see his own mother.

The lieutenant turned to me.

"Any ideas, Joel?"

"Good Lord," I protested. "The thing had a round base—that's all we know. It could be a figurine, a vase—just about anything. You can't tell much from a circle in the dust."

He gave me an impatient look. That's the trouble with pulling too many rabbits out of hats. The first time you bring out a fistful of nothing, you're not just a flop but a saboteur.

"Let's go back down," Ader grumbled. "I want to ask Mr. Zittenfield a few more questions, and we might as well be comfortable."

We trooped down the rickety stairs to the shabby living room.

"What I need from you now," Ader told Zittenfield, "is a rundown on the other people—relations and friends—who associated with your aunt."

"That won't take long," the boy said, seeming a bit more relaxed now that he was no longer personally on the grill. "Aunt Val didn't see many people. She has two nieces, Grace Weinberg and Eunice Mills, who came by once every few months. They live up north somewhere—one in Portland, the other in Eureka, I think. Except for me, they're her only living relatives. As for friends, there's old Mr. de Witt, and Francis Raymond."

"Good. Tell me all you know about these people. Particularly if they're interested in antiques."

"Look, Lieutenant, you're barking up the wrong tree. I know more about that subject than all three of them put together. The two nieces are just nice married girls, wrapped up in their husbands and kids." He spoke with that air of scorn expected of a bachelor. "Their homes are modern and tasteless, judging from the women's descriptions. Any idea of either of those girls killing Aunt Val is just nonsense. Some stranger—a tramp, maybe—must have done it."

"All right," Ader said patiently. "What about the friends?"

"Well, de Witt lives down the street. He's about seventy, but still full of vinegar. I wouldn't be surprised if he was a little sweet on Aunt Val. Anyhow, he was always helping her out with odd jobs—things she couldn't afford to hire somebody for. I gave her a hand, too, now and then, but de Witt is a craftsman, while I'm pretty much of a bumbler. They'd have tea together once a week. She told me he was a perfect gentleman."

"Could he have been angry at her for rejecting him, maybe?"

Zittenfield raised his brows.

"At their ages, Lieutenant? It was platonic; they saw each other, and enjoyed it. My aunt was the fragile, very feminine type a man liked to help. As for de Witt, he wouldn't hurt a mouse."

"That leaves"—Ader peered at his notes—"this Francis Raymond."

"Him!" The nephew was contemptuous. "He has a little real estate office. The only trouble is that every time a Red-Rumped Apparition flies by he's gone like the day before yesterday. One of those real fanatical birdwatchers. The only reason he ever visited with my aunt, I'm sure, is because some rare swallows nest in that clay bank behind the house. He'd talk to her about them, and she'd listen politely, but even if Val could see, she couldn't have told a crow from a pelican."

"This is getting us nowhere in erratic bounds," Ader groaned finally. "I'll have to investigate all these people eventually, I suppose. Come, let's get out of here, Joel."

"By all means," I agreed, thinking unhappily of the work piling up at Pasteur Hospital, which was paying my salary.

We left, leaving Zittenfield sitting there looking pensive.

Once outside, Ader gave Sergeant Briggs, who was pacing stolidly up and back, a few directions, and then took my arm.

"Whoa, boy—not so fast," he said. "I'm going to have a chat with this Raymond character, and you ought to be there."

"Okay," I agreed ruefully. "Just let the appendices and ovaries pile up at Pasteur. I can always work all night."

"I'll let you off seeing de Witt," he said generously, ignoring my complaint. The lieutenant is very single minded.

We didn't find our man at home, but his landlady, a waspish type, told us to try Fisherman's Cove, object a white-haired six-footer. Sure enough, we spotted him stretched out, binoculars in hand, behind some rocks. As we came up, crunching over the sand, he frantically motioned for silence, warning us in an urgent whisper: "Nuts! Nuts!"

At least, that's what we thought he was saying at first, because Ader replied indignantly: "Who's nuts?"

It turned out Raymond was referring to a flock of birds something like sandpipers, called "knots," which are rather rare around this part of the coast. When we introduced ourselves, and finally pried him away from talking about knots, there wasn't much of value he could tell us.

"I was terribly shocked to hear about Mrs. Antoine," he said dolefully, rumpling his snowy mane. "She hadn't an enemy in the world." He spoke in a slow, well modulated voice. This would be all to his advantage if he had anything to hide. When a man pauses after every word, it's hard to spot a more significant hesitation that might precede a lie. It's your fast talker who traps himself most easily, I've noticed.

"Were you ever up in that second floor storeroom?" Ader asked him.

He thought for a moment.

"Once—no, twice. All full of antiques." He paused. "I suppose they could be worth something. Did you consider that point?"

"We did," the lieutenant said dryly. "And are they valuable?"

Raymond shrugged.

"I wouldn't know. Takes an expert to tell." He froze suddenly, snapped the binoculars to his eyes, then put them down with a disappointed air. "Just cormorants."

"There's one item missing from that storeroom," Ader said, eyeing him closely. "I wonder if you happened to remember it."

"Where was it?"

"On a wooden table against the east wall. It had a circular base."

The big man reflected for a moment, then shook his head.

"There was too much stuff," he said. "I guess I'm not very observant." Then, as if to refute this, he called our attention to some dots far out on the surf. "Mergansers," he told us. "Pretty coloring, haven't they?"

"Yeah," Ader said, giving me a baffled look. "Well, if you should recall anything about Mrs. Antoine, or her attic, get in touch with me right away."

I'm not sure Raymond heard him. He had those glasses up again, and was watching a big red-tailed hawk. It was the only bird I recognized that session.

During the next week, Ader and his men did a lot of legwork. Most of what the nephew told us proved to be correct. An expert from Los Angeles explained that the scrimshaw work—carvings made by talented whalers on their long, often boring, voyages—was excellent of its kind, but of interest only to a limited market. A dealer would pay perhaps $300 for the lot. And a well known antique appraiser had a good laugh at the contents of the storeroom. He did concede, however, that today's bad jokes often become tomorrow's treasures; and that by

1980, some of the old lady's horrors might be valuable. He devoutly hoped to be dead by then. Neither of these specialists had any ideas about the missing object, which both Ader and I were beginning to believe held the key to this apparently pointless murder.

Investigation of the victim's relatives and friends didn't help a bit. As Zittenfield had said, the nieces were simple housewives, with nothing to gain from their aunt's death. De Witt and Raymond seemed equally clean. It was more imperative than ever to identify the one object which the killer had bothered to steal. My inability to do this proved most frustrating to Ader. He suggested, in turn, photography, microscopy, x-rays, and chemistry, hoping that one might bring a responsive gleam to my eyes. But all I had to work with was a circle in the dust.

"Let's tackle it from a different direction," I said finally. "First, is there anything our suspects might specialize in that we haven't discovered? Some class of objects, say, which the murderer knows is valuable, but that others overlooked completely."

"If we assume that Zittenfield is competent when it comes to antiques," Ader said, "then the missing item is something else. A round base suggests a figurine; but, damn it, the nephew would know a good figurine when he saw it. At least, he'd remember it was there. This thing, whatever it was, didn't catch his eye. That means it was outside his field of antiques."

"Sounds like logic to me," I agreed. "Assuming, of course, he told the truth. If it was a valuable statue, and he took it, he'd be the last to admit any knowledge of the thing. What does your dossier say about de Witt? Any specialty there? A hobby maybe."

"He collects stamps. But they don't mount stamps on round-based doodads. They use albums."

"Stamps!" I exclaimed. "Maybe we've got something. A whaling captain active, say, in the 1840's, would have used some of the most valuable stamps in the world. Maybe the thing on the table was carried off for a blind, with a bundle of letters the real prize."

Ader jumped up, obviously excited.

"We'll certainly have to check that out. That's the best lead yet."

But we were wrong. There never had been any letters or stamps in the attic. The nieces knew that for a fact, and were able to offer convincing evidence. For one thing, Captain Gray was almost illiterate. For another, Mrs. Antoine had burned all her written mementos when her husband died.

"So that lead is out, too," Ader told me dourly at our next conference. "What other goodies did whalers pick up in 1840?"

"You've got me there," I admitted. "We're up the creek now." I paused. "Eleanor"—she's my wife—"reminded me last night that whenever we've been stuck before, I've always reexamined the evidence, searching for a fresh clue. It's worth a try."

"That's fine—but what evidence?"

"Well, give me all the dossiers, and I'll visit the attic again, just in case."

He rubbed his hands in satisfaction. I knew he saw me pulling the rabbit out of the hat again. And why had I stalled so long?

I went to the house alone. The nephew was out, but Sgt. Briggs let me in with the official key. The storeroom was brilliantly lit by the afternoon sun, and I noticed something we'd missed the other time. The unknown object had stood on a table against the east wall. For ten years the sun had streamed in, and the wall was badly discolored. But each item on that east side had cast its shadow there, so that vague silhouettes were to be seen—areas of unfaded paper, ghostly photographs, you might say.

The outline of the stolen object was fairly clear. Apparently the nephew had goofed or lied, for the shape was at least approximately that of a small statue. It was so grotesque, however, that I thought of a gargoyle. There was no way of telling how much of the distortion was caused by the kind of projection involved. The statue might have been three-quarters facing the wall, or profile.

I made a careful sketch in my notebook. It suggested something familiar, but tantalizingly nameless to me. Then I had it—the outline was that of a lumpish, bird-like figurine. Surely our mysterious object was nothing but a mounted specimen.

That started a whole series of conjectures. Anything might be hidden in a large stuffed bird—letters with rare stamps, jewels, gold coins. Who knows what a smart sea captain could pick up in those days of really free enterprise? Had the murderer sniffed out such a hidden treasure, one that even Mrs. Antoine knew nothing about, and then killed her for it? We knew how well she kept tabs on Captain Gray's stuff, and how unwilling she would have been to sell even a moth-eaten bird. To get it, somebody would have to kill her.

But I was going too fast. In the first place, my identification of the silhouette as that of a bird was in itself a wild guess. I'd taken a survey course in ornithology as part of my pre-med background, but this called for an expert. I thought at once of Francis Raymond, but reconsidered as fast. After all, he was one of the suspects. If there was a hidden treasure in the bird, who would be more likely to find it than a fanatic? The mounted specimen which Zittenfield saw without remembering it, was just the thing to catch the eye of an ornithologist like Raymond. To him, the furniture would be invisible.

I took my sketch to the Los Angeles County Museum, and showed it to one of their experts. When he looked at my crude drawing, I saw his eyes widen. Without a word, he dragged a thick tome from his bookcase, riffled the pages, and gave a little grunt of excitement. I peered over his shoulder, and saw the sketch of a strange-looking, clumsy bird. The caption made me gulp. I expected to read "penguin," because that's what the bird resembled to my inexpert eye.

"Whaling captain," the ornithologist said with growing agitation. "Active between 1830 and 1850?"

"That's right."

"Good God, man, I'm afraid to say it. The Great Auk became extinct about 1844. There's no reason why your captain couldn't have killed and stuffed one."

"Would it have any value?"

"That's the understatement of the century. I doubt if there are more than a few skins and fragments among all the museums of the world. Even a badly mounted one, damaged by insects, would be worth $10,000 at least."

Well, that really cleared the air. Obviously there was nothing hidden in the bird; it was itself a treasure. And only one of our suspects was likely to have known that.

Ader got a search warrant, and we went through Raymond's house and office. We found the Great Auk, carefully cleaned and wrapped, in his garage. Under the lieutenant's relentless grilling, the whole story came out. Raymond had spotted the priceless specimen on his first visit to the attic. He had offered Mrs. Antoine a hundred dollars for it, only to have her refuse. After raising the ante to a thousand, he told her frankly what it was worth, and offered to split in almost any proportion. She wouldn't have any part of selling something the captain had handed down.

Raymond's business was on the rocks, thanks to years of neglect in favor of birdwatching. The temptation was too great. With this foolish old woman out of the way, he could hide the specimen for a few months, "discover" it in some plausible manner, and make a fortune by peddling it to the highest bidder. His only mistake had been in failing to spread fresh dust over that clean circle. Except for that oversight, we never would have known anything was missing, and the murder, without a motive, would have remained unsolved.

As it was, the nephew got $18,000 for the Great Auk. It was in remarkably good condition after a hundred years. I suspect that Captain Gray may have had a few pointers from the distinguished naturalist, Asa.

No Killer Has Wings

I was beginning to think that Lieutenant Ader had finally run out of bizarre cases. He hadn't bothered me for almost six months, or since that "Circle in the Dust" affair.

But I should have known better; it was just a breathing spell. His jurisdiction, mainly the city of Arden, isn't likely to be free of skullduggery for long. Not that I minded too much; in fact, I like playing detective. For that matter, who doesn't?

This was something of a switch, however; because instead of asking me to help solve a murder, it was more a matter of unsolving one first, you might say.

I'm used to being called on by Ader. As the only reasonably well qualified expert in forensic medicine in these parts—I'm chief pathologist at Pasteur Hospital, serving the whole county—I do work for a number of communities in the area. You see, they don't trust their local coroners, since most of them are political hacks long out of practice. So whenever they need a dependable autopsy, especially the kind their man would just as soon not handle—say somebody buried a month—they send for Dr. Joel Hoffman: me.

Last Tuesday I was happily preparing a slide of some muscle section; it had a bunch of the finest roundworm parasites that you'll ever see. Oddly enough, it occurred to me that these organisms, so loathsome to the laymen, were not only gracefully proportional, and miracles of design, but never killed each other through greed or hate, and would never, never build a hydrogen bomb to destroy the world.

Well, think of the Devil—in this case, murder—and he's sure to appear. Into the lab came Lieutenant Ader with a young girl in tow. Him I've seen before, but never in such company, so being a man first and a pathologist second, I looked at her. A small girl, dark, and just a bit plump. What my racy old man used to call a "plump partridge." She had been crying a lot; it didn't need eight years of medical study to tell that. As for Ader, he was half angry, and half ashamed.

"This is my niece, Dana," he said gruffly. "You've heard me mention her occasionally."

I smiled. She fixed her enormous, smoky grey eyes on me, and said: "You're the only one who can help us. Everything adds up all wrong. Larry couldn't have done it, and yet there's nobody else who went out there."

"Whoa," I said. "Back off a few paragraphs, and start over again."

"Larry's her fiancé," Ader explained. "I'm holding him on a first degree murder charge."

I must have looked surprised, because he reddened slightly, and snapped, "I had to, but she thinks he's innocent. Why, I don't know. I've told her about your work before, and now she expects you to perform a Grade A miracle to order. In other words, Dana's picked you to smash my nice open-and-shut case to little pieces."

"Thanks a lot, both of you," I said sardonically. "But I only do wonders on Wednesday and Friday; this is Tuesday, remember."

"That's all right; you can solve the whole case tomorrow," the lieutenant said, giving his niece a rather sickly grin. It was a noble attempt to cheer her up, and of course a complete failure, as such things always are.

"Look," he added, obviously on a hot spot, and not enjoying it, "I've got the boy cold; the evidence is overwhelming. You'll see what I mean in a minute. But Dana here isn't convinced, and to be perfectly honest, I don't see Larry bludgeoning an old man to death for money, myself. He's pretty hot-tempered, but gets over it fast. I don't think he goes in for physical violence, anyhow. Still ..." He broke off, and I could almost read his mind. When you've met enough murderers, one thing soon becomes as clear as distilled water: there's simply no way to tell a potential killer in advance of the crime.

"Why are you so sure he didn't do it?" I asked Dana.

Her round little chin rose stubbornly; I liked her for that. I hate the passive, blonde, doughy kind of girl.

"I know he couldn't kill anybody," she said, "especially an old man lying on the sand. He might punch another fellow his own age, if they were both on their feet, but that's all. Do you think I could love a murderer, and be ready to marry him?"

I looked at Ader, and both our faces must have become wooden at the same time, because she gave a little cry of pure exasperation.

"Ooh! All you men know is evidence. I know Larry!"

The lieutenant is married, and so knows about women. Even so, this line of reasoning, being so feminine, made him wince. But the answer was about what I expected. So I merely remarked: "Suppose you give me the main facts, and then we'll fight about who's guilty."

"Right." Ader seemed relieved. He was always at his best with evidence rather than theories or emotions. I imagine that Dana, in cahoots with his very warm-hearted wife, Grace, had been needling him for hours. Not that he's unsympathetic. I've known cops who wouldn't mess with a case that was all sewed up to please their wives, children, or grandparents. He was doing it for a mere niece.

"First," Ader said, "the victim is Colonel McCabe, a retired Army Officer, sixty-two years old. Yesterday morning, quite early, he went down to his private beach, as usual, accompanied by his dog. After a brief paddling in the shallows, he dozed on a blanket, and while he was dozing somebody came up to him, carrying a walking stick, and calmly smashed his skull with the heavy knob. It seems beyond a doubt that the killer must have been Larry Channing, the colonel's nephew, a boy of twenty-four, who lives in the same house."

"And the motive?"

"Money. McCabe had a bundle. Larry's one of the minor heirs, but fifty thousand or so isn't hard to take at his age."

"Larry's going to be a doctor," Dana flared. "He wants to save lives. And he didn't need the money. His uncle was going to see him through med school."

"That's true," Ader said. "But a quick fortune might tempt even a potential doctor."

"Not only potential ones," I said a little enviously, thinking of the ocean cruiser I'd like to own some day. "But just how did you tag Larry as the murderer?"

"Because the young hothead acted like a complete fool. He left enough evidence—you couldn't call them 'clues'; they're much too obvious—to convict an archangel. Let me show you the sketch."

Here Ader reached into his briefcase, and brought out a scale diagram which indicated the position of the body on the beach and the footprints made by the Colonel and those made by the murderer—to the body, and away from it.

"The sand was quite unmarked to begin with," Ader said, "smoothed out by the tide the night before. We found the colonel's prints, leading from the stairs across the sand to the water, and then back to where he lay down on his blanket. Then there are Larry's tracks from the stairs to McCabe, and back. Nobody else's there except the dog's, which go all over, above and beneath the others. The beach is accessible only from the house and the sea; there's no possible approach at the sides for they're sheer rocky cliffs. That perfect privacy is what makes the property worth $200,000. Now, considering all that, what can any sensible person conclude? McCabe's only visitor, as clearly shown by the tracks, was Larry Channing."

"I suppose you checked all the prints."

"Of course. Although it was hardly necessary. Larry admitted walking out to see his uncle about seven-thirty, while the rest of the family still slept. He even told us that they quarreled again. It wasn't the first time. You see, the colonel didn't want him to marry a poor girl like Dana." A tinge of bitterness came into Ader's voice. As an honest cop, he was always one jump ahead of the finance company. "The old man said that nobody but a fool married except for money, that love was a typically modern delusion, confined largely to soft-headed teenagers and the women who read confession magazines. It's just as easy to fall for a rich girl as a poor one, he maintained. That's how he got his own fortune—by marrying a wealthy widow, no beauty, needless to say. The hell of it is, that gives the boy a better motive than money alone. The colonel was mad enough to cut him off for picking Dana. In that case, no med school."

"Sounds pretty bad. What about the weapon?"

"Well, since McCabe's skull was crushed, we looked for some kind of club. It wasn't near the body, so we figured Larry got rid of it. But blamed if we didn't find it right in the house, at the back of his own closet. It's Larry's pet walking stick, an ebony one with a roughly rounded, heavy knob for a handle. It had been carelessly wiped. There's still some blood and hair on the thing. Now isn't that a stupid way to commit murder?"

At that Dana leaped up, her eyes blazing. "He didn't do it, that's why! Don't you see it's too obvious, too easy?"

Ader grimaced.

"I've thought of that," he said, "and in a way I agree. Unless he hoped to make us think that way—to believe he was framed, and very crudely at that. Larry is a bit hot-tempered, as I've said, but no fool. And only a prize idiot would leave a damning trail like this one. Talk about painting yourself into a corner. This bird put on a dozen coats."

I had been studying the diagram while Ader talked, and now I groaned. "It was sure to happen some day. I might have known."

"What's that?" the lieutenant demanded.

"I'll tell you. If Larry is innocent, you've got a real classic here—a locked room murder, basically. The tracks on the sand show plainly that nobody else came anywhere near the victim. Are you positive he was killed by a blow from that stick?"

"Not yet, although I'd bet on it. But there's been no autopsy yet, and the stick hasn't been tested by a pathologist. All we've done so far is check fingerprints and tracks. They're all Larry's and the colonel's. The rest is up to you. But the man's skull was dented badly, so if anything else killed him, the blow was superfluous, which makes no sense. However, the body's at the morgue; I'll have it brought here. You can have the stick any time, too."

"What about Doc Kurzin? Going to bypass him again?" Kurzin's the coroner, an ancient incubus who missed his forte as a meat-cutter for some supermarket.

"I'll have to, if we're going to get anywhere. Your standing as an expert in this county gives me that right, officially."

"All right," I said, a little reluctantly, because to be honest, it seemed that the boy must be guilty. After all, most murders are not subtle; they are chock full of blunders. When a man is keyed up to the point of killing, he's not likely to be a cool planner. "I'll do the p.m. as soon as you get the body here to the hospital. Then, if you want to bring the stick later, I'll see if the blood and hair are really the victim's. Meanwhile, do the usual and make me one of your fine lists of suspects. You know, descriptions, character analysis—the works. You've a knack for that."

"There are plenty of possibles," Ader said glumly. "Four other heirs in the house, and I don't think the colonel ever won any popularity contests in the army or out of it."

"How many of the other suspects fly? Because, believe me, it'll take wings or teleportation to explain how the old man got killed without the murderer leaving tracks on the sand."

"That's why I can't help thinking Larry did it. I don't want to believe it, but the alternative, as you say, means a parachute jump, or something. And," he added in a bitter voice, "a similar jump in reverse—upwards."

"Larry is innocent," Dana said firmly to me. "If you remember that, you'll find the explanation. You're our only hope, Dr. Hoffman, so please try very h-hard."

"I should warn you of one thing," I told them, "I'm not an advocate, remember; I can't take sides. What if the facts of my investigation—" I was going to say, "—put another nail in the boy's coffin?" but had the good sense to hunt a different metaphor—"make the case against Larry even worse? Maybe you should give the job to Kurzin at that. He'll mess it up so that the jury might give the boy all the benefit of the doubt."

"You won't hurt his chances. He didn't do it, and that's what the evidence is bound to show finally," Dana said, her voice still firm.

Ader shrugged in half humorous resignation.

"You heard her," he said. "I'm inclined to agree that there's nothing to lose, really. The worse D.A. in the business couldn't fail to get a conviction right now, with no further investigation." He led his niece gently towards the door. "I'll have the body brought over immediately. And I'll drop by myself with the stick later, unless I get tied up somewhere." He patted the girl's shoulder sympathetically, and they left.

Watching Dana leave, chin up, I thought that if Larry was smart enough to pick her, he wasn't likely to bungle a murder so badly. Then I thought my logic was getting worse than hers, so I went back to my roundworms.

The body arrived about ninety minutes later, and things being slack at Pasteur, I was able to get right to work. Beginning, as usual, with the head, I had to agree with Ader that the crushed skull certainly explained the man's death. In addition, it was also true that the old boy was remarkably healthy otherwise, and could have reached a hundred. There were laborious tissue and toxicological tests possible, but I felt them to be counter-indicated. I had no doubt he was killed by a blow to the head. I was just finishing up these gross tests, when Ader came in with the walking stick.

He studiously avoided looking at the remains, even though everything was back in place. In another minute I was through, and covered the body with a sheet. Then Ader came closer.

"Well?" he demanded.

"He was killed by a clout on the head, all right. Let's see that stick."

He gave it to me. There was a plastic bag over the heavy end of the stick; the stem was thin, tough ebony, thirty-eight inches long. There was little doubt that egg-shaped handle could account for the bone injury. Whether it had or not remained to be seen.

The blood test was fast and simple, a matter of typing the blood. The hair didn't take long either, using a good comparison microscope. I shook my head ruefully at the results, and Ader's face was bleak. He had his tail in a crack, so to speak. On the one hand, he had a dream of a case, with none of the usual rat race of finding reluctant witnesses and other sorts of elusive evidence. On the other there was his niece, Dana, a favorite relation I inferred, about to lose her beloved to the gas chamber, or, if they were lucky, to a prison for thirty years or so. Either way, the lieutenant wasn't going to be happy. Unless, of course, we found a new candidate for the big jump.

"I'm sorry," I said. "This is no help. McCabe was killed by this stick. I'll stake my professional reputation on that—and will have to so testify under oath."

"I wasn't expecting anything else," he said listlessly. "For Dana's sake, I was only hoping. Anyhow, here's that complete rundown on the rest of the household. Read it over tomorrow, and maybe you'll think of something. You've done it before on more hopeless cases."

"This one out-hopelesses all the others," I said. "And frankly, we don't need suspects as much as we need 'how was it done.' One murder; one rather obvious killer—what's the point in additional names?"

"I don't know," he said wearily. "But begin by assuming Larry is innocent, and then figure out how somebody else might have done it."

"Very simple," I replied. "All I need is another month and fifty per cent more brains. But I'll try, Master."

Ader left, looking desperately tired. He probably hadn't slept much since the murder.

It was after eleven, but I didn't feel pooped at all, so I sat down with the family dossier. Ader is very good at this sort of thing, and I could easily visualize the members of Colonel McCabe's household.

There were five in the family itself, exclusive of the dead man. They were Larry, the nephew, a boy of twenty-four; two sons, Harry, aged thirty-two, and Wallace, thirty-nine; the colonel's brother, Wayne, fifty-seven; and a cousin, Gordon Wheeler, twenty-eight. As for servants, an elderly couple kept the place clean and did the gardening. A middle-aged woman did the cooking.

When it came to motive, they all had it, except for the servants, who were provided for whether the colonel lived or died. For the family, it was a matter of money. McCabe was worth well over a million, his late wife having been the childless widow of a rich manufacturer. The colonel's will was no secret. The two sons were down for $200,000 each; the brother, $150,000; Larry, $50,000; and the cousin, $30,000, all tax free. After a few small annuities to the servants, anything Uncle Sam left would go to the local museum, provided they kept McCabe's arms collection, all of it, on permanent display.

For the old man fancied himself a military expert of high order. But instead of refighting the Civil War, and the one in 1914, he preferred to correct the errors of earlier generals. In short, he intended to rewrite Oman's "The Art of War in the Middle Ages."

One room of the house was devoted to a collection of medieval arms and armor. This was the responsibility of the cousin, Gordon, who catalogued the stuff, and kept it so polished and functional that McCabe could have left on a crusade at any moment, perfectly equipped with plate armor, sword, lance, dagger, and crossbow. Only a horse was lacking.

The late colonel was something of a bully at times, but not really a bad sort. There was no evidence that he interfered unduly with the members of his family, or that any of them had serious cause to hate him. It seemed to me, reading between Ader's lines, that the only reasonable motive was money. For McCabe was possibly a bit stingy on handouts, although everybody had an allowance of sorts.

But, actually, motive wasn't the basic problem here. My real job was just as I'd stated it to Ader: If Larry didn't kill the colonel, *how* was it done? The "who" could wait, and would probably come from the method, I felt sure.

I took out the diagram and photos again. There's a process called "brainstorming," very popular on Madison Avenue. It consists of throwing the rational mind out of gear, and letting its motor race. You give your wildest fancies free rein, hoping to find gold among the dross. I tried that, and came up with some weird notions. The craziest was a theory that the murderer wore shoes giving fake pawprints of a dog. The trouble with that was the obvious shallowness of the prints on the photos. The coach dog weighed perhaps sixty pounds, this weight distributed over four paws. A 160-pound man would leave suspiciously deep prints by comparison. Still, I meant to have Ader check on the actual depth of the prints. I was desperate, you see.

But that "solution" didn't even convince its inventor, so I took another tack, and this one gave me a thrill of hope. What if the approach had been from the sea? According to Ader's notes, all members of the family were water-skiers, and the like—why not skin divers, too? If the murderer came out of the water, with or without special equipment, killed the colonel, and returned the same way, would he have left tracks, or would the tide erase them? Here was a very tenable possibility.

I was tempted to ring Ader at once, but it was after twelve, and I remembered his weariness. Wednesday would be soon enough. So I went home to bed, and dreamed of a skin-diving coach dog that terrorized the bathers.

The next morning I phoned the lieutenant, and told him my two theories. The man walking like a dog, as I'd feared, was nonsense. The plaster casts—this surprised even me, but Ader leaves nothing to chance—showed them far too shallow to have been made by a man.

The second solution, about approach from the sea, however, did excite him. The only question was whether such a feat was possible at the private beach. One way to settle that was to check with Sammy Ames, sports editor of the local paper, a buff on water games. Ader gave him a call, while I listened in, conference style. Ames was very emphatic. Nobody unwilling to commit suicide would swim within five miles of that coast at this time of the year. The undercurrents made it physically impossible to survive there; not even an Olympic gold medallist could manage it.

That was bad enough, but a call to the Yacht Club brought further verification, plus the fact that some footprints would have been left, at least until the evening tide came in.

It was hard enough finding those two theories; now I had to come up with a third, and it had to be a better one. That made a visit to the house mandatory, so I asked the lieutenant to take me there.

The place was quite impressive: a big, roomy, two-story mansion, with stairs in the back leading down some sixty feet of rock to the private beach. That beach was bounded with those minor precipices on three sides, and the sea itself on the fourth.

I won't waste time describing the family, since their physical qualities are not relevant. All the men were healthy, athletic types, strongly masculine. They seemed genuinely sorry for Larry, but certain he was guilty.

The collection of medieval arms would have made the visit worthwhile in less harrowing circumstances. The walls were lined with daggers, battle-axes, bills, pikes, crossbows, and other ancient man-killers. There were several dummies in full suits of armor, beautifully burnished. Wheeler, the curator of this family museum, was obviously proud of the collection, and had become a trained specialist on medieval warfare through his research for the colonel. He enthusiastically demonstrated the correct use of several outlandish weapons, handling them with the assurance of an expert.

But none of this was clearing up the mystery—if there was one, and Larry didn't happen to be our murderer.

Well, I was pretty discouraged at this point. Maybe John Dickson Carr can make up and solve these locked room puzzles on paper, but this was too much for me. I was ready to throw in the sponge, and go back to Larry as the killer.

But then I recalled other recent cases Ader and I had worked on. In those, a fresh appraisal of the evidence broke the impasse. Besides, I liked Dana. And it makes a difference, when you have a personal interest in an investigation.

So back I went to the lab. The first thing I did was re-read my notes on the autopsy. They didn't change a thing. The colonel's skull had been fractured just above the right ear. I tried to visualize how the blow might have been struck. If the killer had stood to the right of, and just behind the old man, lying there with his feet towards the sea, and made a golf-like swing from the right to left, with the knobby end of the stick down, hands near the ferrule, that would account for the injury. Nothing unlikely there; no inconsistencies to take hold of.

Rather gloomily, I turned to the remaining evidence, the stick itself. I held it in the way I had pictured it, and tried to reenact the fatal swing. Suddenly I felt a surge of hope. The blood and hair were in the wrong place! If the stick had been swung, like a golf club, by a standing man, the side should be stained. In fact, that would be true no matter how the thing was manipulated as a bludgeon. But instead, the very top of the handle had the blood and hair. How was that possible?

Excited, I experimented again. The only way to hit a person with the top of the knob would be to make a spear-like thrust forward with it. But that would be awkward and unlikely even if enough power was possible, something I doubted. Then a whole new prospect opened before me, one that suggested many significant modifications of our interpretation of the evidence. That stick hadn't been used as a club at all. It must have been projected like a spear, knob first. But how? Certainly nobody could actually throw the thing, like a lance, with suffient force and accuracy to kill a man from—how many feet? I checked the drawing again. The body was almost forty feet from the foot of the stairs, which is where the murderer would have had to stand in order to avoid tracking up the sand. Such a throw was utterly fantastic by sheer muscle power. The skull has thick bones, not easily fractured.

Then, looking at that long, slender body of the stick, I had an idea. I grabbed my lens and studied the metal ferrule. Sure enough, there were two shallow but definite grooves across the tip. They could have only one explanation; in them a taut string would not slip off the end of the ferrule. That meant a crossbow—it seemed obvious, now. What could be simpler than placing the narrow ebony rod in the slot of a strung crossbow, knob forward, and then, from a position on the stairs, aiming at the man lying there on the sand. The stick, propelled with all the force of a powerful metal leaf spring, would strike a terrific blow on the victim's head.

I began to pace the floor feverishly. A perfect solution; one that explained everything. So that's why there were no other tracks. The killer didn't need to leave the stairs. What no mere arm could do, the crossbow made easy. Aiming one was no harder than pointing a rifle, and forty feet was a short range. Even so, the murderer must have practiced a bit to make sure. Perhaps he hadn't hoped to convict Larry, but merely to confuse the issue.

All right, he shot the strange arrow, then leaving it by the body—I cursed. Another good theory gone to pot. The stick had not remained by the corpse. How did the marksman recover it without leaving tracks?

I thought of a string, say a nylon fishline, tied to the missile. But another peek at the photos ruined that solution. There was no long, narrow trail in the soft sand to show where the stick was hauled back.

But I knew there must be some explanation; the rest fitted too well. I examined the stick again, starting at the ferrule. In the middle of the polished stem, I found some indentations. They were not deep, but then the wood is very hard. I measured them, and noticed their spacing. There were no others like them; obviously, Larry took good care of his prize possession. It was baffling, especially because I felt that I was getting close.

Then, seeing the photo again, it came to me. The sort of thing I should have spotted immediately. But any theory needs testing, so I called Ader, and asked him to meet me at the beach. He was to get, on the Q.T., one of the nonsuspects, say the housekeeper, to bring Gustavus Adolphus, the coach dog. I wanted somebody the animal knew, and would obey. Since she fed him, that was no problem. He knew and obeyed her.

At the beach, I showed Ader the marks on the stick, and explained the crossbow theory.

"Those marks have been made by teeth," I told him. The Dalmatian was racing about, happy to be out on the beach again for a romp along the shore. At our request the housekeeper, a little bewildered but willing, stood on the stairs and flung the ebony stick end over end towards the water. "Fetch, Gustavus!" she shrilled, and barking joyously, the spotted dog raced out, seized it with his mouth, and carried it to the woman.

I grinned at the lieutenant.

"That completes the story. When the old man was dead, and the killer stood where she is now, all he had to do was shout 'Fetch!' and the dog retrieved the murder weapon. A wordless accomplice. Neat. No footprints on the sand."

"He was sure a lot of help to the poor colonel," Ader snapped, giving the clumsy hound an indignant glare. "Instead of chewing up the murderer, he helps the guy get away with it. Or almost."

"Don't blame the dog," I said. "You can't expect these so called lower animals to understand murder. That takes the higher intelligence; the same that invented it. But Wheeler must be our man; as you saw, he's an expert on all those medieval weapons. Now that I think of it, he didn't demonstrate or even discuss the crossbow. That's pretty significant."

"I've no doubt that's the way it happened," Ader said. "Now to prove it to a jury."

"That won't be easy," I said. "Except for the grooves for the bowstring, and the teeth marks on the stick, there isn't any evidence to impress laymen. I can't prove the stick was actually fired. Maybe we haven't helped Larry very much, even now."

"Don't you believe it," was the grim reply. "I know just how to break Wheeler down. The oldest trick in the game. He'll get an anonymous phone call tonight. Somebody will describe the main points of the murder, claiming to be an eyewitness, and demanding a payoff. If Wheeler's guilty, and I've no doubt about that, he'll want to meet that Mr. X very badly, either to bribe or kill him. We'll have him cold, with witnesses. But first, we'll have to see that the housekeeper doesn't spill the beans. Luckily, Gustavus Adolphus can't talk."

"Don't say that. If he could talk, our job would have been a lot easier."

Well, as Ader promised, the trap worked. I can see why. A murderer is full of fears generally, and the worst of them is an eyewitness to the crime.

Dana says that she and Larry will name their first boy after me. I suggested Gustavus Adolphus instead. Although he was an accomplice, he finally testified for the defense, making our case solid.

A Puzzle in Sand

I've never met a more conscientious cop than Lieutenant Ader—and that's just as well. If there were any more of his kind in these parts, I'd have to quit my job as Chief Pathologist at Pasteur Hospital, since there wouldn't be enough time in the day to serve two masters.

The trouble with Ader is that he won't bring a case to the D.A. until the sheer weight of the evidence would sink a nuclear submarine with all hands. And if there's a medical angle, that means calling on me— Dr. Joel Hoffman. Sure, there's a coroner available officially, but the old boy graduated back in the days when surgeons operated in frock coats and carried sutures in their lapels.

A few months ago I helped the lieutenant solve that murder on the beach, the one that fitted the classic "locked room" problem. Now, by a really wild coincidence, here he was back with another mystery killing on that very same stretch of sand. What's more incredible, it had the same pattern in many respects. You see what I mean? Only with a guy like Ader could anybody run across not one, but two, locked room stinkers in the same place.

You must recall the set-up. A private beach, with sheer cliffs on three sides, and the ocean on the fourth. A big house on the bluff opposite the water, with stairs leading down to the sand. Anybody who goes from the house to the sea leaves tracks; and the tide produces a clean slate each night, so that the sand is unmarked almost every summer morning.

You'd think that anybody with enough grey matter to cover the head of a pin would find a better place to kill a man. It wouldn't be much worse to do it at police headquarters, and then sign a confession in six languages. But then, maybe I'm just fed up with that jinxed private beach, and wish that a tidal wave would erase it so that I could concentrate on other matters—the kind for which Pasteur pays me.

Well, the first I know about being in for a reprise of the last case, I look up to see Ader standing there with a face as long as one of those ten-second commercials on TV.

"I've got another impossible stinker on that same McCabe beach," he moaned, "and a hundred-carat heel to pin the murder on. I ought to be happy; it'll look great on my record, and yet I just can't buy it."

I knew immediately that whatever I'd hoped to accomplish for dear old Pasteur in the next few days was going to be sidetracked temporarily. When the lieutenant's in that mood, the only way to get rid of him would be so drastic as to ruin our friendship, which is unthinkable. So I gave him a seat—not the rigged one that keeps a visitor sliding off, but a comfortable, rump-sprung armchair.

When Ader outlines a case, you have to admire that computer brain of his. The facts come out like toothpaste from a tube—smooth, shining, sort of linear. You can almost visualize the subheadings of the report.

It was certainly a weird business, coming as it did in exactly the same place as our last case together. After the death of Colonel McCabe, his big house and private beach had been rented by the heirs to a Myron Crane and his family. They were already well known in the community. Crane was a banker, civic leader, philanthropist, elder of the church—the works. Sharing the house with him were a younger brother and two of Myron's children, Sylvia and Brian.

Well, one morning Ader receives a call from the brother, David, that the older Crane was lying dead on the beach, apparently from a gunshot wound. The lieutenant took charge in person, hurried over, and found things exactly as stated. There was Myron Crane, a bullet through his right temple, stretched out some forty feet from the stairs. From a distance, you'd have thought he was just relaxing in the sun. Aside from his own, one-way tracks, there were those of only one other person, which led out to the body and back. It seemed an obvious case of murder committed by somebody with the I.Q. of a retarded baboon. The killer might just as well have tied himself to the corpse and fired a three stage rocket.

On questioning Dave and the children, Ader quickly found a prime suspect. The night before, Myron Crane had quarreled violently with a visitor, a man named Garrison, who called on the banker occasionally, at home, in regard to some confidential business matters never discussed with other members of the family.

It was all so obvious that Ader had the willies. The tracks on the sand came from Garrison's shoes; and the murder weapon, a P-38 war souvenir, was discovered under the rear seat of his car. His fingerprints were not on the gun, but after all even the worst amateur can't make every possible mistake. Apparently, Garrison had remembered to wipe the butt clean.

"Aside from that," Ader said, "it was perfect. We had the motive—that quarrel; the opportunity—an isolated beach; and proof of the murderer's presence at the scene of the crime—the footprints."

"Then what's the problem?" I demanded. "You should have every case so easy."

"How many perfect, textbook measles victims do you get in medical practice?"

He had me there. Half the time the patients lack two-thirds of the official symptoms. Same with appendicitis.

"You see," the lieutenant said. "Garrison screams he's been framed, and anything this pat certainly suggests it. Ordinarily, I wouldn't take much stock in this particular beef; it's just what anybody caught in such a spot would claim. But here's the part that bugs me. Garrison admits he was blackmailing Myron. It seems he was a bailiff, when the old guy got involved in a stock swindle in Chicago fifteen years ago. A lot of poor people—don't laugh—widows and such, lost plenty of dough. It was a cheap, dirty kind of business, and Crane was convicted under another name. He did a short stretch, too. It's the kind of rap that doesn't look good on a banker and church elder, even if reformed completely. Well, a victim may murder a blackmailer, but not the other way around. That's like burning your own savings."

"Not always," I objected. "Suppose the old man was desperate, and intended filing criminal charges against Garrison."

"Believe me, it's never done. Besides, with all payments in cash, Crane didn't have any evidence to convince a jury. Garrison was too cagey to put any threats in writing, or to make them with witnesses around. Remember, he found his pigeon after twelve years, which is a long time to wait. Crane was ripe; and Garrison certainly must have been determined not to make slip-ups."

"Yet there were witnesses to the quarrel the night before the murder."

"Yes, but only to the yelling and exchange of blows. The family didn't have any idea what the two men were fighting about. Their conversation before that was very quiet, and behind locked doors."

"All right. But if Garrison didn't kill Crane, who did? And why the frame?"

"That's just the point. Garrison swears the old man committed suicide after the ante was raised."

"Then what was Garrison doing out there on the beach? And why didn't he report the body before David did?"

"There's the frame, he says. He claims that somebody phoned him in the morning, quite early—about eight—pretending to be Myron Crane, and urging a meeting on the beach. The imposter—if he was one—sounded rather like the old man, but spoke of having a touch of laryngitis. Apparently it worked, because Garrison wasn't suspicious. The bait was a cash settlement of fifty grand to buy him off for good. No wonder Garrison didn't bother about the voice. There isn't a blackmailer alive who wouldn't jump at such a chance. He could grab the cash and still come back for more any old time. Great sport, blackmailing."

"Then Garrison's story is that he was deliberately lured into leaving those tracks. But why didn't he go right to the police with a report of the suicide?"

Ader displayed a trace of disgust at my denseness.

"You guys with clear consciences," he snorted. "It's obvious. As soon as Garrison got near Crane, he saw the guy was dead—shot—and not having clean hands, he panicked. Besides, not being a fool, he saw that the sand marked him as the only other person on the beach. That could mean plenty of trouble if the death didn't happen to be suicide."

I digested those facts for a moment, then said, "If Crane did kill himself, how did the gun get in Garrison's car?"

"Brother, that's what I'd give my pension to find out. It's the one thing that makes stale hash out of his story. He doesn't even remember if the gun was actually in Crane's hand, or somewhere nearby on the sand. But he sure denies carrying it off. Yet there are no other tracks out there. A guy would really be nuts to remove a suicide gun in such circumstances. It ruins his only defense."

"Wait a minute. Why should there be other prints? You could shoot a man in the head from as much as a hundred feet—at least, any good shot could."

"Sure, but not with powder burns on the skin. That gun muzzle was not more than six inches from Crane's head. I'm no pathologist, but I dig powder burns real good. And from the stairs to the body is almost sixty feet."

"Would anybody else have a motive for killing him?"

"I suppose there's always a motive for anybody. Crane's brother and the children inherit quite a lot of money—nothing spectacular, say $130,000 in good stocks. But whether they wanted it badly enough to commit murder—who can ever say?"

"There's one thing," I said, "that tends to support Garrison's story to some extent. You said there was only one set of tracks other than the victim's. The brother—David?—goes out to the beach, sees Myron lying there, and without even walking over, decides he's dead—murdered? That's not a natural reaction. It smells like a trawler full of fish to me."

"My fault," the lieutenant said, a little sheepishly. "I left out a few details. First of all, David heard that one shot at about eight-thirty. It didn't bother him because his brother often used to toss those Christmas tree ornaments—the light, colored, bubble type—in the surf, and pop at them with the P-38. But when there were no other shots fired, Dave thought it rather queer, and went out on the balcony for a look. It's about a hundred yards or so, down at an angle, from there to the beach. The house, you remember, is on a bluff. Well, seeing his brother lying there, so still, he wondered, especially after that single shot. It was a bit too far for the naked eye, so he went in for his binoculars, a sixteen power pair. With them he could make out the whole business quite clearly—the bullet hole, even. Some people might have rushed down and trampled up the sand, ruining all the tracks, but he kept his head and phoned me, staying off the critical area."

"Sounds reasonable—if a bit cold-blooded, for a man who's just lost a brother."

"Let's be fair. We keep reminding the public not to mess up the evidence at the scene of a crime."

"Yes, but how could he be so sure his brother was dead?"

"Oddly enough, that bothered me, too, so I asked him. He said that although the hole in Myron's temple was convincing enough, the main thing was the body itself. After serving in two wars, he told me, there was no mistaking a corpse. As we both know, he's right; there's a certain slackness, a crumpled doll look, that tells the story. All very logical, yes?" He gave me a quizzical, almost pleading glance.

"You mean," I said grimly, "that it's just a bit too logical. But, on the other hand, why are you trying so hard to give this lousy blackmailer a break? It seems to me that the facts are more than enough to take care of him, so why look for loopholes? His story might conceivably be true, but all the evidence points another way."

"I didn't expect that from you," Ader said, sadly reproachful. "It's just what Garrison hopped on me for. In fact, he got almost hysterical. Said that because he was a blackmailer, I was willing to see him executed for a murder that didn't happen. There was just enough truth in the accusation to hurt a little. I wasn't certain he was guilty—you see why; the whole thing's much too tidy—but wanted to take the easy way out. What the hell, I thought, a blackmailer is lower than a murderer anyhow, especially if the killing is hot-blooded. There's nothing more cold, cruel, and calculating than holding some poor devil's past sins over his head while you suck him dry."

"So," I cut in dryly, "your Calvinistic conscience began to work overtime, and you decided that just because Garrison was a muck-worm, you'd try for a more airtight case than it would take to convict an archangel in heaven."

"The swine has one of those pink, bland faces," Ader said irrelevantly, "like something over-ripe that's just been peeled. I loathed him from the start."

"Therefore, he must get a square deal," I said. "I dig you all the way. I'll see what I can do. Just leave me some photos of the scene, and when you get a chance, send me your usual lucid notes on the people involved. And, so help me, if we ever get this mess straightened out, better put that confounded beach off limits—it's jinxed."

"I'm with you there," he said fervently, and left.

When Ader had gone, I decided to begin with what was handiest—the photographs. They brought back memories of the last case, all right. There was the isolated beauty of a beach, with cliffs on three sides. From the huge, old-fashioned house steep stairs led to the yellow sand, and from them, needle sharp in the enlargements, I could see the one-way tracks of Crane and the two-way passage of Garrison. Except for those three lines of footprints, the surface was relatively unmarked. It was clear, in any case, that nobody else had walked there the morning of the tragedy.

But there were other traces. I couldn't be sure what they were, but knew better than to ignore them. I had learned, from my association with previous cases, that in crime, as in medicine, one must be alert for the most minor indications. One of the marks was not so small, either; it was roughly five by eight inches, but not, of course, rectangular; just a disturbance of the sand-grains. It was roughly twenty feet from the body, more or less in line with the stairs. There were also several much smaller traces on the surface. I took them to be tracks of gulls, since they seemed to show something suggesting furrows made by small toes. Perhaps they had no connection with the case at all, but since they lay along that critical line from body to stairs, I couldn't afford to be complacent about them. As a great admirer of Freeman's Dr. Thorndyke, I heartily subscribed to his axiom about collecting all the evidence, even when its significance was not apparent.

Unfortunately, after puzzling over all these marks, I still didn't have any idea what they meant. So after an hour, I gave up on the pictures, put them aside. Luckily, just about then, a patrolman came in with Ader's notes on the people involved in the killing. At least, those he knew about.

The victim, Myron Crane, was fifty-seven, and, as explained earlier, a pillar of the community. Except for that one black mark in his salad days, he had led a blameless life. An ideal blackmail target. He had no known enemies, and was on excellent terms with his two children and brother, David. The latter was fifty-three, and sold real estate, handling the financing through Myron's bank. Both men were normal, except perhaps for the lack of women in their families. The elder was a widower, and the younger separated from his wife. They were known as hard workers and enthusiastic sportsmen. Myron liked to shoot; David preferred fishing, especially trolling for the yellowtails in the open sea around Catalina. According to people who knew them well, the two brothers were very close, almost neurotically so, which might explain why neither had remarried.

Myron's children were twenty-seven and twenty-nine. The younger, Sylvia, was a legal secretary; Brian was a dentist. Both lived at home, but the girl was engaged. Brian was still playing the field.

It would seem that all four members of the household were quite successful in their chosen careers; they had satisfactory bank accounts; and if there was any reason for the brother or two children to murder Crane, Ader hadn't been able to root it out. After all, they lived with Myron rent free, and usually even ate his food. The man had been more than generous.

I should mention that there were a few servants, but they had nothing to gain from the death of their master.

One point in Ader's notes was interesting, strictly from the romantic angle. The Cranes' descent, on their mother's side, was in direct line from a famous hanging judge of the frontier, a Roy Bean type character. I don't know why the lieutenant bothered to record that, except, as I implied, because of an un-police-like taste for the nostalgic glitter of the past.

Well, none of these facts helped much. All they did was make Garrison a better bet than before, since he had at least fought with Myron Crane, while the family got on with the old boy famously. But I could see Ader's point, too. A blackmailer isn't likely to kill his pigeon while it's still fat and juicy. Maybe in self defense, or after it's broke, but not otherwise.

So I was stumped again. It was getting to be a familiar feeling. Anyhow, by now I knew the drill. Keep plugging away. There was one obvious step first. I should take a look at the body, even though this particular case didn't seem to revolve about the manner of death. So I had Ader take me to the morgue for a change.

Unfortunately, thanks to Dr. Kurzin, the ancient coroner, the body was chilled to the consistency of those cube steaks you find at the very bottom of a supermarket's freezer. But that didn't matter too much; I wasn't attempting anything as detailed as an autopsy. It was quite clear that the cause of death was a bullet which passed through the right temple and emerged behind the left ear, leaving a large exit hole.

"We had a helluva time finding that slug," Ader said. "Must have been twenty feet to one side of the body. Still, that's better than having to get Kurzin to probe for it; he'd end up around the navel."

I looked at him sharply. It wasn't like the lieutenant to pull such a howler. "Good God!" I said. "That's rather important. If Crane was shot by somebody standing over him, while he lay, or sat, on the sand, the bullet would be much closer. Finding it that far off seems to support the suicide theory. If you're sitting on the ground, and put a gun muzzle to your right temple, the slug comes out at only a slight downward inclination, and could go a dozen feet or more before hitting the sand. It's not conclusive, of course, but—"

"—but I'm an idiot!" Ader said. "I shouldn't have missed that one."

"It may not be too important," I soothed him, examining the rest of the body. When I had made a fairly casual survey of all the external marks, there wasn't much to go on. There was nothing whatever abnormal about the corpse except for some rather curious scratches on the right hand. I pointed these out to the lieutenant, who grunted.

"That doesn't mean anything," he said a little dolefully. "I told you Crane quarreled with Garrison. They exchanged a few punches. Probably Garrison's teeth damaged Myron's fist."

I'm ashamed to admit it, but at the time that explanation got by me.

"I've been thinking," I told Ader. "If we assume Garrison is telling the truth, and Crane really did kill himself, then the gun you found in the car must be Myron's. In that case, Garrison would be in a better position with the jury. At worst, it might mean that Crane had his own gun with him, there was a struggle, a continuation of the earlier one, and Garrison shot in self defense."

"It's not that simple," Ader said. "You don't give me credit for much brains. A couple days later I searched for Crane's own gun at the house, and there it was. So he wasn't killed with his own gun at all. Odd, though, two P-38's being involved."

"They're pretty common, I understand. Still, it is pushing a coincidence pretty far."

"Don't I know it!" he flared. "Why do you think this case has me chewing the draperies? The D.A. would think I was crazy to even question the evidence, but you understand how I feel. It's too slick, as if somebody's putting on a puppet show for our benefit."

"Well, there's nothing more I can do here," I told him. "We know what killed him. Our problem seems to be who did it, if Garrison didn't. And above all, how was it done without tracking up the sand?"

"Go back to Pasteur and think it through," Ader said. "Maybe you'll pull another rabbit out of that microscope."

"You're getting that thing confused with Aladdin's lamp," I objected.

He drove me back in the cruiser, and I figured I might as well do a little work for the hospital. Ordinarily that means rather intense concentration on the job at hand, but this time the chore was routine, so I could let my mind range freely over the murder case. It's strange how while you're walking, or doing something automatic, you can sometimes get on top of a problem that's baffled you for days.

I began with the notion, however far-fetched, that Crane had shot himself that morning, there on the beach. He would probably sit down, hold the gun to his right temple and shoot. The slug could certainly go a number of feet and bury itself in the sand. He would topple and, like most similar victims, retain the gun in his clenched fingers. But it might drop to his side; nothing is certain in these matters.

All right, along comes Garrison, lured by that fake call promising a big cash payoff. The body isn't so unnatural as to tip him off while he's yards away; besides, he's gloating over the money. But then from a few feet away, he sees that Crane is dead, gets scared, and scoots.

I looked at the photos again. Possible confirmation: the tracks away from the body were clearly those of a man in a big hurry; the stride was longer; the tread heavier; the grains more widely scattered. But he'd be in a big rush if he'd killed Crane, too. So his eagerness to get away from the body, didn't necessarily prove Crane a suicide.

Still, those return tracks were consistent with the idea that Crane was dead before Garrison arrived. Very well, he finds the body and runs, leaving Crane there, a P-38 in his hand, or beside him. What about a suicide note? Garrison certainly wouldn't carry that off, thus really sticking himself with a murder rap. Either there wasn't any, or—for that matter, it could have been left in the house. But then, why didn't the family produce it? Surely Crane wouldn't leave it on the beach without a stone or something on top to keep it from blowing away.

But none of this was as vital as the question of the gun. Whoever framed Garrison simply had to get rid of that P-38 by the body. Actually, he'd done better—planted it in the blackmailer's car. But how? Nobody else had been near Myron Crane out there. You couldn't deny the testimony of the sand.

I tossed the pictures aside, disgusted with myself. In spite of all this impeccable reasoning, I still hadn't the foggiest notion what had really happened that morning on the beach.

I made some strong coffee over a Bunsen burner and read through the dossiers again. I was looking for some way of retrieving a handgun sixty feet out on the sand. Then, all of a sudden, it came to me. The truth has a clear ring to it, like an honest silver coin. At the same time, I had a mental image of Crane's scratched hand. What an idiot I'd been, accepting Ader's explanation. Those fingers had never been bruised against Garrison's teeth; even a first year med student should have caught that, for those cuts were made after death.

I was sure of my case now, but equally positive it would never stand up in court. The kind of evidence I had was not only circumstantial, but the finicky tenuous sort that meant worlds to a lab man, but nothing whatever to a housewife or clerk.

Well, I'm a pathologist, not a policeman, and what I did next is no part of my job. Nor would Ader approve. But I called on David Crane at his real estate office. It was clear that people weren't standing in line to buy houses, so I had him to myself.

"So you're the distinguished pathologist, Dr. Hoffman," he said pleasantly, when I'd introduced myself. "Lt. Ader mentioned that you wore working on the case, although I can't imagine why, since there's no doubt about any part of it."

"That isn't quite so," I replied. I liked the man's looks. He had one of those squarish, almost ugly faces that often go with a candid, generous character. But the eyes were of that type of blue that can chill to polar ice.

"But surely Garrison's guilty. The evidence is overwhelming. The man's walled in."

"Yes, but I'm the man with the pick."

"Meaning?"

"Meaning that I know what really happened."

He didn't reply to that; but just sat there, sitting back quite relaxed. So I went on, trying to jar him.

"Your brother committed suicide, of course. I infer he was tired of being bled by Garrison."

David Crane had excellent nerves, but I'm a doctor and saw one cheek muscle twitch convulsively. There was also a pulse throbbing suddenly under his right ear.

"What did you do with the note?" I demanded. "Burn it?"

"I've no idea what you're talking about," he said in a level voice. "Just tell me your conception of the killing, so I'll be able to follow."

"Gladly. Your brother went out early to the private beach, probably about seven-thirty. He left a note somewhere in the house—probably by your door—and took his P-38 along. He sat down in the middle of the sand and shot himself through the head—hence the powder burns and the position of the slug.

"You heard the noise, didn't like the sound of that one shot with no further firing, and got up. You must have found the note, read it, seen what a filthy leech had done to your brother, and decided almost immediately to frame him if possible. Through the binoculars you verified your fears, and the sand gave you the key idea. If Garrison could be lured out there, what with no other tracks around, he'd be tagged for the killing. The family would testify about the quarrel, thus establishing a solid motive. So you phoned him, pretending to be Myron. Most brothers sound at least a little alike, and he fell for it. After he panicked and ran, you thought he was really on the toasting fork; but right away something must have occurred to you that gave you a nasty jolt. There was that gun in Myron's hand—or was it alongside the body? In either case, it might just clear Garrison. You had to retrieve it. But obviously you couldn't just walk out there, leaving tracks and messing up your perfect case against Garrison." I stopped to catch my breath, and David looked at me in a sort of wonder.

"You're a remarkable man, Doctor. Why don't you write science-fantasy?"

"I couldn't see how it was done, at first, but those marks on the sand, and the scratches on your brother's fingers—made after death, you see—they were the clues. And the lieutenant's fine dossiers, of course. I'm no expert on this part," I went on, staring him straight in the eye, "but you'd want a fairly heavy lure. I'd use a strong, surf-casting rod, say seven feet long, and a twenty pound line. Something like a one ounce South Bend Surf Oreno. It shouldn't be too hard to snag a P-38."

This time Crane laughed outright; it was almost a shout of relief.

"By George, Doctor—you've named the exact lure, so help me! But you forgot one point, which luckily I didn't. If you wouldn't file the barbs off those hooks, and snagged anything but the gun, that would be the end. It was a break, my catching his hand only once, and not the clothes. But that's because I made shorter trial casts first."

"I know," I told him. "That accounted for those marks I first ascribed to gulls. They were made by the lure striking the sand and being whipped back. The one bigger depression must have been where the gun landed after your first tug."

"Dead right again. It simply wasn't possible to bring several pounds of P-38 to the stairs in one pull, and I certainly couldn't just drag it along the sand without giving everything away. After my first try dropped it somewhere between, I had to hook it again. Then one more yank brought it to the stairs where I was standing."

"What about the gun Ader found in your house—the other P-38?"

"It's not hard to find a dozen—all untraceable, brought home during the war and never registered. You'll never know the old buddy I got it from. I had to work fast, knowing your lieutenant would get around to looking for Myron's gun in a few days after Garrison screamed frame-up."

We studied each other in silence.

"Well?" I said.

"Everything's very well. The swine's going to the gas chamber. Neither you, nor Ader, nor the Court of Last Resort is going to save him. Nothing that I've admitted here will be repeated at the trial—it's hearsay evidence, and I'd deny every last word."

"You don't have to worry about being punished; I'm sure Ader won't press charges. Temporarily unbalanced by the loss of your brother."

He gave a mirthless laugh.

"I'm not in the least worried about the law. Nobody can prove a thing on me. I want the hide of that blackmailer, and I've got it. There's nothing anybody can do to stop me."

The hell of it is, he was right about that.

"I could say something about 'Vengeance is mine, saith the Lord',"
I began a bit sheepishly, preaching being out of my line. "But more to the point, will you be able to live with yourself knowing that an innocent man was going to die because of your shenanigans?"

"There's no such thing as an innocent man, only those less guilty. This one deserves to die, and he will, believe me."

His face was set like stone, and all at once I seemed to see that ancestor of his, the grim and terrible hanging judge. I felt sure that some of those genes were showing up in David Crane.

I'll tell Ader all about it, but, frankly, I don't think there's a thing he can do.

Birds of One Feather

"The dead man I can understand. The dead parakeet is what bothers me."

I looked up from the microscope. Lieutenant Ader hadn't brought me one of his weird cases for several months. No, that isn't a fair way to put it, either. The fact is, I'd been discouraging him a bit lately. Work had piled up at Pasteur Hospital. I'm the pathologist there—Dr. Joel Hoffman. So when Ader had tried to get me involved a few times earlier that year, I'd squirmed out of it by showing him all the jobs they'd lined up for me in the lab. Then, naturally, he wanted to avoid pestering me. Now I felt a little guilty; I like the lieutenant, and quite often in the past we'd made a good team. He uses me as a sort of scientific consultant—without pay, I might add, but that part isn't his fault. The coroner, whose function I was so blithely usurping, didn't care; he was on salary, a fat one. The lieutenant loves to bypass Dr. Kurzin anyhow, since the old boy is not exactly a Spilsbury. In my book he should be cutting meat for some supermarket.

Now I turned on my stool, snapped out the microscope lamp, and said: "Okay, tell Poppa more about it."

"It's just as I've been saying. They found Horton dead by his car, apparently about to change a tire that was almost flat. Death turned out to be due to cyanide poisoning."

"Who said so?" I demanded.

He looked sheepish.

"Kurzin, I'm sorry to say."

I shook my head in disgust.

"Be reasonable, Zee. How the devil can I work on a case when the p.m.'s been done by that idiot? For all we know, the victim died of acute dandruff!"

"Don't exaggerate," Ader snapped. "I could smell the bitter almonds myself. There was nothing tricky about that part. Besides, old Kurzin had a bright med student—his nephew—helping out; they both said it was definitely cyanide. Seems to be no question."

"Lord help us—another generation of Kurzins coming to louse up future crime detection. All right," I added hastily, as the lieutenant showed his impatience at that irrelevance. "Let's assume for once he got it straight. What's your complaint, then?"

"Well," he said unhappily, "maybe I'm just looking for trouble, it's such a minor matter. But why the dead bird?"

"You mean the parakeet they found with him?"

"Yes. He always took it along. It perched on his shoulder; you know how they are. So the guy finds he has a flat, and gets out to change it. Then and there—how I can't imagine—he takes, or is given, cyanide, and dies in a few seconds. Must have been a big dose, because he collapsed right there, and never budged. But why the bird—and how?"

"I don't see the problem. If he was given, or took, some poisonous food, he must have let the bird have a nibble. What's so odd about that?"

"Kurzin says Horton's stomach was empty; no food at all. He certainly didn't eat before starting on the flat; there were no traces of anything—I mean bags, garbage, that sort of stuff."

"There are other things he might possibly have swallowed."

"Very true; in fact he did take some aspirin. Kurzin found traces in his stomach."

"Well," I said, "if a person wanted to kill somebody with cyanide, what better way than to add it to the victim's aspirin? It would be easy to mold some into a tablet that looked just like the harmless ones. The salt is white, you know. This way, too, the murderer could be miles from the spot, with a good alibi."

"Yeah," he said in a gloomy voice. "That was the consensus of my brilliant colleagues, but I can't buy it. My instinct says there's something wrong. You see why, I'm sure."

I considered the situation for a moment, then stood up.

"I think I do. It doesn't quite add up. The dead parakeet spoils the picture. A man might let the bird peck at his apple, or a cookie, or even the lettuce from his sandwich; but who feeds aspirin to a parakeet?"

"Exactly the point," Ader said, his brown eyes shining. "Now take it from there. How was this guy given poison in such a way as to kill the bird, too, and without leaving any food either in his stomach, or at the scene of the crime? I've been wondering about that for days, but can't come up with an answer that makes any sense. That's the only reason I'm bothering you again, with all that work on your hands. You have a knack for seeing through these puzzlers I run into."

Part of that was the old oil, of course; but the two of us had figured out a few tricky ones together.

"I suppose the autopsy specimens are gone by now."

"According to the state law," Ader reminded me, "Kurzin didn't have to keep 'em—only swear to his findings; you know that."

"Too bad. If he and the med student goofed, we'll be following a false lead."

"You could go over the report," Ader suggested, and I groaned. Reading one of Kurzin's official documents gave me the same feeling an editor would have if forced to plough through a handwritten manuscript submitted by a near illiterate.

"All right," I agreed reluctantly. "Have it sent over. Maybe, at that, it can't be much worse than 'Sixty Six Sunrise Square'." I'd planned to watch that show on TV in the evening; don't ask me why, unless it's because the program can be followed with only two per cent of the brain cells without missing a single cliché. That's very useful, and makes for fruitful meditation. The answer might emerge.

Well, that night I went over Kurzin's report, which was more incoherent than usual. But he did have the facts on cyanide poisoning fairly straight, no doubt because it's so common only an idiot could miss. There was obvious corrosion of the gastric mucosa, and similar traces of the nasty stuff in other parts of the body. I inferred, unhappily, that having found the poison in Horton's stomach, Kurzin hadn't bothered looking much further. There was no estimate of relative distribution to the brain and other organs at all. With what he had, plus the bitter almond smell, he wasn't the kind to poke around; that might hold up the poker game.

So when Ader came for my reaction, I wasn't able to tell him much.

"It seems to be cyanide, all right," I said cautiously. "But about the parakeet, I'm no better informed than when we began. Why not try another angle? How about motive? If you find out who had that, the method might be clear."

"There's always motive," he said in a weary voice. "Hell, if I found Albert Schweitzer dead, it would turn out he had fifty enemies! In this case, it's a lot worse. Insurance, for example; he had twenty thousand dollars worth in favor of his wife. Then there's revenge. You see, he was a loan shark—need I say more? No? Well, I will. This guy never let anybody off the hook. *But* if you were a pretty gal, the payoff didn't necessarily have to be in cash. Now, I ask you, if you were a husband, and found that your wife was in the tender clutches of a guy like Horton, and that maybe she'd paid off without cash, how would you feel? Motive? Brother, I could almost murder the swine myself, and I never even met him alive!"

"Tell me again about how they found him."

"A passing motorist saw him sprawled by the car on the shoulder of the road. Being a bright fellow, he phoned the highway patrol."

"You're sure he didn't mess up any evidence?"

"Positive; he had good sense. All right, the highway boys radioed me, and I found Horton dead, lying by the right front tire. He'd removed it, and was about to put on the spare. The bad one had a slow leak; made by a nail, I'd say; anyhow, it was almost flat. The way we figure it, he was going along the El Toro road, minding his own business like the other vultures in the area—only they're honest, legitimate ones; the kind that fly—when he realizes the tire's down, and pulls over. He gets out, tweetie bird on one shoulder, jacks up the front tire, and removes the wheel. He gets the spare, and is about to put it on, when the poison begins to work. That cyanide is very quick, I understand."

"It depends on the dose, but on the whole, yes; there's nothing much faster."

"At least the sequence of events is simple," the lieutenant said, as if searching for a comforting thought. "No fancy timetable; no guesswork. A child could reconstruct exactly what happened there. If it wasn't for that damned bird ..."

"Without the parakeet, you'd say he got the cyanide with his aspirin, I presume."

"I suppose so," he agreed halfheartedly.

"Look," I told him. "Let me think about it all for a while. We both know that sometimes the pieces fall in place if you poke away at them for a few hours. Maybe it'll seem very simple by tomorrow."

He brightened. "That's what I was hoping you'd say. You always have worked that way. Remember that goofy horse-collar murder? And the old woman with her attic full of junk?"

"Don't remind me; they almost sprained my headbone, as Pogo might say. Now get out, and let me think."

He left, rubbing his hands hopefully. Ader has a lot of faith in me. Sometimes I think he forces me to perform over my head, if you know what I mean. But in this case, things were different. I didn't have data of my own, but had to depend on somebody rather incompetent. For all I knew, Horton's stomach might not have been really empty. For example, if he'd eaten a couple of peanuts, and given his pet a few, Kurzin might have missed the small amount of food involved. Then I remembered that the lieutenant had checked the scene for food, and found nothing. On his own grounds, Ader is unbeatable; if he didn't find any food, there wasn't any around.

I studied the police photo of the dead man. Like all official enlargements, it was sharp; a horrible technique for a glamor portrait, but ideal as evidence.

There was Horton, a chubby fellow who might have been somebody's benevolent uncle by the look of him. His face was badly contorted, naturally; cyanide is potent stuff; it may be fast, but time is relative, and there are easier deaths, which take longer. Beside him was a pathetic bit of fluff that was his parakeet. No doubt he'd been fond of the bird. Another case of loving lower animals and hating the "higher" ones, our fellow men. The Nazis had been like that. Maybe it isn't so crazy to prefer birds to people; but then a loan shark is least qualified to look down on his fellow men.

The dead bird obtruded itself again. Without it there was no puzzle about how—only who.

I went back to the report. Maybe the bird hadn't been poisoned at all. Suppose somebody had just strangled it to confuse the police. My idea didn't pan out, though; they had found no marks of violence on the tiny body; and Kurzin claimed cyanide caused that death, too.

Then I began to think about birds in general, hoping to find a useful line of attack. They have their own peculiar weaknesses; they are light and fragile, with hollow bones. Otherwise, flight would be impossible. A bird can be frightened to death very easily; its metabolism is high; it runs a perpetual fever. Canaries are highly sensitive to dangerous fumes; in mines they are used—or were—to detect fire damp and similar deadly gases.

And at that moment, it was as if a flashbulb went off in my brain. The pieces fell together, and I knew the solution was very close. It had to be right. And if so, there was still danger for innocent people; right now somebody could be near his death. I got on the phone fast.

"Zee," I said hurriedly. "Where's the car Horton was driving? The one in the police photo."

"Still in our garage—impounded. Why? You sound excited. We went over it very carefully—what did we miss?"

"Never mind that now. Call them, or radio, whatever you do, and make it clear nobody is to mess with that car. They should stay far away. Maybe even evacuate the garage. Got it?"

"What's it all about? Don't be so damned mysterious."

Perhaps I should have given him a hint over the phone, but I had a sudden urge to spring it all at once, dramatically. Too much TV, maybe.

"Meet me there in twenty minutes. I may have the answer we need."

"I hope so," was his fervent reply. "There isn't even the right question at this end."

At the big police garage, Ader led me to the car.

"How did it get here?" I wanted to know. "By towing?"

"No; that wasn't necessary. The sergeant finished putting on the spare, and then he drove it back."

I gave a low whistle.

"Lucky fellow. He could be as dead as Horton, if my theory is correct."

"What do you mean by that?"

"I'll tell you. And I'm so sure this must be it that I won't even cheat by testing my solution in advance before sounding off. The dead bird was the clue, just as you thought, genius. You know, it's not easy to tell poisoning by hydrogen cyanide gas from the kind caused by a salt—say, potassium cyanide. I'll bet anything that Kurzin and his nephew missed the significant differences by not checking the nose and lungs carefully."

Ader gaped at me.

"You mean Horton was gassed? That nothing went into his mouth?"

"Yes."

"But that's impossible. He was out there alone; no signs of a struggle. Nobody's going to hold still for an execution."

"Tell me, among the suspects was there anybody in the exterminator business? You know, bugs?"

"Well, we checked all the people on our list for their possible ways to get cyanide. We found a photographer; he uses the stuff to tone pictures—he says."

"That's right; they do."

"Then there's a metalworking foreman; his plant uses pounds of the chemicals. Let me see." He fished out his work notebook. "Hm. One guy does have a brother-in-law who works for the 'Bug Out Company'—what a name! But why him? What about the first two?"

"You miss the point; they don't use gas, and exterminators often do—in tanks, under pressure."

"You trying to say somebody brought out a tank of cyanide gas, and gave Horton a face full right on the road? How would they know he was going to stop, unless …"

"Hold that last thought; it's correct. About that stop, I mean. But no tank, no murderer on the spot was needed. Let me lay it out for you.

"Horton is driving along, when he finds his front tire has a slow leak—made by the killer, that's for sure. All right, he pulls over, gets out the spare, and prepares to change wheels. My guess is he notices that the spare is very hard—it would have to be obviously much over-pressured for the victim not to miss it—to take the bait. What would you do in that case?"

"I'd let some air out."

"Exactly what Horton must have done. He reached over, pressed the valve, and releases a big blast of what he assumes is air. He doesn't stop to wonder how the tire got that way, or maybe he does; but who would suspect the real truth? Anyhow, it isn't air at all, but cyanide gas under high pressure, fed right from a tank of the stuff into the tire. A tiny whiff would be plenty; Horton got a whole cloud; and the bird on his shoulder enough to wipe out an aviary."

Ader shook his head. "Holy jumping Jerusalem—" he began.

"Let's check it out," I said, "before we rejoice too much. Stand back, and I'll let out a smidgeon of something or other from the right front tire. It's lucky for that sergeant of yours that Horton brought the pressure down to about normal with his one fatal blast, because otherwise you'd have another corpse." Here I gave the valve a tiny push, then very carefully fanned the air above it, urging some towards my nose. The bitter almond smell was unmistakable.

"That's it, all right," Ader said, sniffing in a gingerly way. His eyes narrowed. "The killer must be connected with Horton's garage. Nobody else could have doctored a tire that way."

He turned out to be right about that. A mechanic at the garage had a pretty sister, whose husband worked for the exterminator. He had been in a bad way financially, after a severe illness; and his wife, in despair, had gone to Horton for money. The loan shark had given it to her, and then tried for payment in other coin than cash, finally terrifying her into submission. His kind know how to frighten people. But her brother, the mechanic, found out what happened to his sister, and decided to remove Horton for good. It was easy for him to borrow a tank of cyanide from the brother-in-law's plant.

I was hoping he'd get away, out of the country, but Ader's too quick and careful. All the killer said when they booked him was: "I'm sorry about the little parakeet, but it shouldn't have teamed up with a vulture. 'Birds of one feather flock together'."

Checklist of Sources

Note: The checklist below gives the original publication source for each of the stories included in this collection.

"Dead Drunk"
Alfred Hitchcock's Mystery Magazine, December 1959

"Horse-Collar Homicide"
Alfred Hitchcock's Mystery Magazine, January 1960

"Circle in the Dust"
Alfred Hitchcock's Mystery Magazine, February 1960

"No Killer Has Wings"
Alfred Hitchcock's Mystery Magazine, January 1961

"A Puzzle in Sand"
Alfred Hitchcock's Mystery Magazine, February 1961

"Birds of One Feather"
Alfred Hitchcock's Mystery Magazine, January 1963

About the Author

Arthur Porges was born in Chicago, Illinois on August 20, 1915. One of four brothers, he was educated at Roosevelt High School and Senn High School before enrolling at The Lewis Institute where he achieved a Bachelor of Science Degree in Mathematics. After the successful completion of his postgraduate studies, through which he attained Masters Degrees in Mathematics and Engineering from the Illinois Institute of Technology, Porges enlisted in the U.S. Army in 1942. During the Second World War he served as an artillery instructor, teaching algebra and trigonometry to field personnel. He was stationed at various military installations including Camp White in Oregon, Fort Sill, Oklahoma, Camp Roberts, California and at Barnes Hospital in Vancouver, Washington. After the war Porges returned to Illinois and taught mathematics at the Western Military Academy, going on to serve as an assistant professor at De Paul University. Having taught at Occidental College in Los Angeles for a brief stint in the late forties, Porges made a permanent move to California in 1951 and spent several years as a mathematics teacher at Los Angeles City College. During this period he wrote and sold short stories as a sideline. In 1957, Porges retired from teaching to write full-time. He went on to publish hundreds of short stories in numerous magazines and newspapers. Many of his stories appeared in *Alfred Hitchcock's Mystery Magazine*, *Ellery Queen's Mystery Magazine*, *Amazing Stories* and *The Magazine of Fantasy and Science Fiction*. His fiction spanned several genres, with tales ranging from science fiction and fantasy to horror, mysteries, and so on. At his most prolific his work was appearing in three or four periodicals in one month alone. Among his best-known stories are "The Ruum," "The Rats," "No Killer Has Wings," "The Mirror" and "The Rescuer." Eleven previous book collections of his short stories have been published: *Three Porges Parodies and a Pastiche* (1988), *The Mirror and Other Strange*

Reflections (2002), *Eight Problems in Space: The Ensign De Ruyter Stories* (2008), *The Adventures of Stately Homes and Sherman Horn* (2008), *The Calabash of Coral Island and Other Early Stories* (2008), *The Miracle of the Bread and Other Stories* (2008), *The Devil and Simon Flagg and Other Fantastic Tales* (2009), *The Curious Cases of Cyriack Skinner Grey* (2009), *The Ruum and Other Science Fiction Stories* (2010), *The Rescuer and Other Science Fiction* Stories (2014) and *Unusual Plants of the Galaxy* (2014). A keen birdwatcher and an avid reader, in later years Porges wrote many articles, essays and poems, most of which were published in the *Monterey Herald*. Several of his poems were collected in the book *Spring, 1836: Selected Poems* (2008). After spells in Laguna Beach and San Clemente, Porges moved north, eventually settling in Pacific Grove. He passed away, at the age of 90, in May 2006.